THE GULL WORKSHOP
AND OTHER STORIES

THE GULL WORKSHOP

AND OTHER STORIES

LARRY MATHEWS

Breakwater Books
P.O. Box 2188, St. John's, NL, Canada, A1C 6E6
www.breakwaterbooks.com

A CIP catalogue record for this book is available
from Library and Archives Canada.

ISBN 9781550819731
COPYRIGHT © 2023 Larry Mathews

We acknowledge the support of the Canada Council for the Arts. We
acknowledge the financial support of the Government of Canada through
the Department of Heritage and the Government of Newfoundland
and Labrador through the Department of Tourism, Culture, Arts and
Recreation for our publishing activities.

Printed and bound in Canada.

Breakwater Books is committed to choosing papers and materials for
our books that help to protect our environment. To this end, this book
is printed on a recycled paper and other sources that are certified by the
Forest Stewardship Council®.

Canada Council   Conseil des Arts
for the Arts   du Canada

Newfoundland
Labrador

Canada

For the members of the
Burning Rock Collective

CONTENTS

THE GULL WORKSHOP

Old guy who runs it doesn't give his name. Doesn't give a reason, just prefers it that way I guess. Only four of us have showed up. Me, Tommy Giordano, Jack Littrell, Ziggy Jasinski. We're all old guys too, come to think of it. Not that we'd describe ourselves that way. No women present. I mean they'd be allowed to come, it's not that, but they're just not interested. For whatever reason. But don't get me wrong. If they wanted to be here, they'd be welcome.

Anyone take this workshop before, the old guy wants to know. I raise my hand, sort of tentatively. It's been such a long time. Truth is, I've pretty much forgotten what it was all about. A gull workshop. What does that even mean?

The poster was pretty vague: Gull Workshop, Saturday Afternoon, Usual Place. What exactly is that supposed to convey?

I don't think Tommy, Jack, and Ziggy have much of a clue. Why are they here then? Why am I here, for that matter.

You, the old guy says, looking at me. You've taken the workshop before, but you don't remember much about it, right? Doesn't matter because this one will be different. They're all different. I nod, because I think that's what he wants, some response, but a minimal one, not one that leads to real back-and-forth.

They're all different, he says again, slowly. They're. All. Different. Like it's some grand but understated revelation about the nature of the human heart. Or something. Just a tad too dramatic for my taste. I sense that the others are getting a little restless, anxious for things to start moving.

Then Tommy speaks up. Sir, he says, Are you going to tell us what this is all about? I mean, a *gull* workshop. It's such a weird phrase. I mean, what are we going to *do*? Does it have anything to do with actual gulls? I don't see any in here. So, like, what's the story?

I'm thinking the old guy might be offended by this, but he just smiles and says, Mr. Giordano, you're Mr. Giordano, right? What do you think it's all about? What would you like it to be all about? Please answer and then I'll call on Mr. Jasinski and Mr. Littrell.

And then you, he says, looking at me. I'll call on you last. Since you've done this before.

Okay, Tommy says. If you really want to know. What I'd like it to be "all about" is a trick question, isn't it? I mean, *you* know what it's going to be all about since you're running it. So why don't you tell us? Tommy is no dummy. He speaks softly. He's not confrontational. Look, we've all agreed to come here for a workshop, so why not spill the beans?

The old guy says, Mr. Giordano. Please. His posture informs us that he's being very patient.

Tommy waits a few seconds, appears to be experiencing some sort of internal turmoil, which he's struggling to overcome. Knowing Tommy, I'd say it's probably all fake. Good guy at heart, but a bit of a ham. Of course we all know he's had his troubles. Know a bit too much about those troubles, truth be told. Those facial contortions designed to express distress, I'd bet he's practised them in front of a mirror this morning. No matter what the workshop turned out to be about, he'd find a way to do his thing.

Okay, Tommy says finally, Here's what I was thinking. Please pardon me if this seems naive. Or just stupid. I figured, like we'd come in, and you'd have a bunch of blocks of wood, gull-sized blocks, let's say, and you'd pass them out and give us some spiel about how in each of those blocks of wood there's a gull just waiting to emerge if we did the right things. You know, like the gull is in there already, fully formed, alive. In some sense. Know what I mean?

So it's like we'd be in a parable or something. A parable? And then you'd show us what to do with the blocks of wood, like maybe some woodworking trick, maybe with chisels or something. Or maybe exotic tools we'd never seen before. And maybe we'd also have to say appropriate words, maybe in a language we'd never spoken before.

And then, when we'd done all that, a gull would fly out of each block, would maybe assemble in some elaborate pattern near the ceiling. And you'd say something like, See guys, you're all in a parable about creativity or ingenuity or imagination or something like that.

And then we'd go home and say to everyone, Hey, we're all in a parable. And of course by then you'd have set the gulls free, and they'd fly away, and there'd be no way to prove that any of it had happened. But we'd still be in the parable. The parable would be real. We wouldn't have to write it up or anything. That's the kind of thing I was hoping for.

He stops then, looks down at his shoes. Embarrassed that he's given away too much.

The old guy waits until it's obvious that Tommy isn't going to say anything more.

Then he says: Thank you, Mr. Giordano. It was very kind of you to answer my question in such detail. But no, that's not what the gull workshop is "all about."

And you, sir, he said, looking at me. It's quite remarkable how blue his eyes are, how intensely he stares. I've seen that before, once, years ago. But the person turned out to be disappointingly ordinary, nothing to write home about, as people used to say. In the days when people actually wrote home.

Yes? I say. I decide not to tack a "sir" on to the end of my question. After all, he's an old guy, I'm an old guy, why should I be deferential to him?

You've taken this workshop before.

I say that I have.

And you remember little about it?

Correct. Almost nothing.

Okay. But you're starting to remember now, aren't you? Not everything, but certain things you and the other guys did, is that not right?

And it is. I'm starting to remember a few things, though I'm not sure how to describe them. So I nod.

I want you to know, he says, all of you to know, that I'm not different from you. It's not as if my experience of life, or my understanding of life, has been superior to yours. I just happen to have a knack for running these workshops. A knack is what it is, best way to describe it.

Then he stops and takes a sip from his water bottle, swishes it around in his mouth—I *guess* it's water, no telling what it could be, none of my business anyway—then swallows, a little too much drama in the gesture for my taste. Maybe a bit too much like Tommy would do it. But so what.

Puts the bottle down, clears his throat, looks up at the ceiling, stained tiles. Starts to talk.

Like all of you, he says, I too have known success and failure, love and loss, been rebuked and scorned, "'buked and scorned" as the old spiritual has it, been unfairly treated and treated others unfairly. I've seen the best and worst of the human condition. Just like everyone. Including everyone here.

Like everyone? I'm thinking I might say something now. Have I myself, for example, personally witnessed the best and worst of the human condition? Probably not. Most of what I've witnessed has been pretty mediocre, to be honest.

I raise my hand, and the old guy sees it, but he won't let me speak. I suspect you're going to ask, he says, whether what I just said can be true. Mr. Giordano? Is that what you're wondering?

Tommy looks up for maybe the first time in a while. He's losing patience, I can see. But when he speaks, he's back in his "voice of reason" persona, speaking slowly and distinctly, and maybe a bit louder than necessary, given that we're all in this one small room.

What I was wondering, he says, was what all this has to do with gulls. I mean, when does the actual workshop get started?

Now the old guy smiles, hard to describe that smile. Sort of *benign*, I guess you could say. Not condescending, not like he's looking down on us or anything. It's kind of a life-affirming smile, meant for all of us, collectively. That's the sense I'm getting, anyway. Maybe a little too much kumbaya in it. But nobody asked me to judge.

Now you tell me, Mr. Giordano, he says, does this have anything to do with gulls? Yes, Tommy says, yes, I believe it does. That was a bit of a surprise. But then Tommy goes on: And that was what I was wondering. You're right about that.

Now the old guy is speaking again. Yes, he says, it is true. Best and worst. Everyone. Though some forget. Or try to. Know what I mean?

You're beginning to understand what we're doing here now, too, aren't you. Mr. Littrell? Mr. Jasinski? Jack and Ziggy both nod.

And you? he says to me.

I think Tommy wants to say something, I say, because I can tell Tommy is bursting to speak.

I think I get it now, Tommy says. At some point we actually *become* gulls. Right? Of course after that we can be human again. Right? Because who'd want to be a gull permanently? I mean, what sort of life would that be? Am I on the right track? In the ballpark?

No, Mr. Giordano, the old guy says. Now he's grinning. No one is going to become a gull. Not even for a minute. The rest of us laugh, a little uneasily, at this. What if we find out later that we've all been thinking that?

Oh, says Tommy. Crushed. I just thought that if we became gulls we'd still have the parable thing going for us. Wouldn't we? I mean, I haven't had time to think it through or anything. That's all. I mean, I know it's a stupid idea, but.

No, Mr. Giordano, the old guy says. It's not a stupid idea. Not at all. It is, however, the wrong idea. This is not a parable. This is reality.

So, he says. Are we ready now? Mr. Littrell? Mr. Jasinski? Mr. Giordano?

Ready for what? I think of saying, but then I realize it won't be necessary. The old guy is staring at me again. Fiercest blue eyes you've ever seen.

You, he says, it's all coming back, isn't it? And it is, stronger than before. Perhaps, he says to me, you can tell the others what to do next.

I can. And I will. And so we get down to it.

THE DEATH OF ARTHUR RIMBAUD

t came as quite a surprise to us to learn that it was Arthur Rimbaud, the famous poet, who'd rented the old farmhouse on the other side of the river. He'd been here for several months before we found out who he was, I mean that he was famous, and then it was only by accident. One of the kids at the high school—it was Dave Hutchinson, Bill's son—came across the name on some random website. He told Dick Delacroix, the French teacher. Delacroix had never heard of any poet named Rimbaud, but he did some checking, and soon we had the whole story. Rimbaud himself had never said a word about it.

Of course, some of the details were hard to swallow. For one thing, Rimbaud the poet was supposed to have been born in 1854, which would make him over a hundred and fifty, but our Rimbaud didn't look a day over thirty-five. Then there was the fact that the poet was supposed to have had his right leg amputated, and the Rimbaud we knew had both his legs. And the poet was supposed to have died in 1891. When the story about him started going around, most of us more or less suspended judgment.

None of us knew Rimbaud too well, although he seemed a pleasant enough person. We didn't see much of him at all. Even though the farmhouse he lived in was only two miles or so up the road—we still think in miles around here; the metric never really caught on—he never came into town more than once a week. He used to drive a pickup, an old blue Chev. At first we thought maybe he didn't trust the old covered bridge that crosses the river. It's perfectly safe, but every time you drive across, it feels like it's going to collapse, and sometimes strangers are pretty leery of it. Finally one week somebody asked him if that was it, and he said no, that didn't bother him at all, it was just that he liked his privacy. He was like that, never volunteered any information, but if you asked him something, he'd tell you without hesitating. Not that anybody asked him much. We believe in minding our own business. Even so, when we saw him buying his supplies or driving off in his truck, we couldn't help but wonder what he was doing out in the farmhouse, all by himself, week after week.

He made it clear right from the start that he didn't want to be bothered. I think it was November when he moved in, around the time of the first snow. At the end of the month, Harry Graves, his landlord, drove out to collect the rent. Harry was a bit annoyed when he found the gate padlocked. He had to climb over it and walk the hundred or so yards to the house. He said later that Rimbaud was polite, but obviously not too happy to see him. When Harry asked him about the lock, Rimbaud said he was worried about prowlers, which was ridiculous. We don't have problems like that around here, and anyway, there's hardly ever any traffic on that road. Harry said he explained all this very carefully, but Rimbaud didn't really seem to be listening. The other thing that put him off, he said, was that Rimbaud kept him standing in the hallway instead of inviting him in. From what Harry could see of the front parlour, it looked like it'd been turned into a chemistry lab. Or who knows, maybe a meth lab, Harry said, not that anyone around here would know what a meth lab was supposed to look like. There were wooden benches Rimbaud had apparently made himself, with fancy pieces of equipment made of metal and plastic. Bunsen burners, test tubes filled with strange-looking liquids. A funny smell about the place too, Harry said. Rimbaud was quite evasive about the whole thing. He said he was doing research of some kind for a book he was going to write. Harry let it go at that. Afterwards, Rimbaud made arrangements to leave his rent money at the post office, so Harry wouldn't have to drive out to the farmhouse.

On Saturday afternoons, Rimbaud used to stop at the British Arms for a few glasses of draft beer before going home. One time just after the story about him being a famous poet had become common knowledge, some of us invited him over to sit at our table. He seemed a bit reluctant—nobody'd ever asked him to drink with them before, not because people didn't like him but because he seemed to prefer it that way. But he did come over. It was Baxter Martin who asked him, point-blank, if he was *the* Arthur Rimbaud, the great poet. Without batting an eye, Rimbaud said yes, he was. He loosened up a bit after that, at least compared to what he'd been like before.

Before long we'd asked him the other questions that's been bothering us. Baxter said what about being born in 1854, and Rimbaud said that at the age of thirty-five or so, he'd just stopped aging, it was as simple as that. There were reasons for it, but he couldn't go into them now. He also said both the amputation of his leg and his death in 1891 had been faked, something he did because there was an insurance policy he wanted his mother to collect on. He'd felt bad about it at the time because he didn't like to be deceitful. But he knew by then he wasn't going to age anymore, and his mother had this life insurance policy on him, one with double indemnity in the event of loss of limb before death. He wouldn't have done it if she hadn't needed the money badly.

Clyde Dunbar, who's an insurance agent himself, said he'd never heard of a policy like that. When he said it you could see the hurt look in Rimbaud's eyes. But then Baxter asked Clyde sarcastically if he'd made a study of life insurance in nineteenth-century France, and Clyde said, well, no, he hadn't, and Rimbaud brightened up again. A few minutes later he excused himself, saying he had things to do at home. After he'd left, Steve Adams remarked that he had an honest face. Nobody disagreed.

Life in this town wasn't quite the same after that. You have to understand that nothing much has ever really happened here. No famous old-time explorer ever passed through this part of the country. There've been no battles, no acts of heroism, nothing we can look back to with a lot of civic pride. It's been this way forever. The industries are farming and lumbering. Kids grow up, work, raise families. We've never had a boy win the Victoria Cross or make it to the NHL, or a girl who became a movie star or had quintuplets. The only local political issue is the bridge, and that's pretty dull. Even though we know the old covered bridge is safe, most of us think we should have a new one, something that looks halfway modern. A lot of politicians have made promises about it, but nothing ever gets done. But when you come down to it, probably nobody really cares that much about the bridge. It gives us something to argue about, and that's as far as our interest in the subject goes.

So when the Rimbaud thing came along, it had quite an impact. Not in the commercial sense: it was only Joe Summers, the proprietor of the British Arms, who thought of making money out of it. And his plan to build a motel to accommodate visiting Rimbaud enthusiasts didn't come to anything. The rest of us never thought in those terms at all. Instead we started to get excited about the poetry itself. Dick Delacroix was the first. He had a friend in the city send up a volume of Rimbaud's poems, and reading it was like a conversion experience for him.

He could hardly talk about anything else. The funny thing was, the people he talked to got just as excited, without having read a line themselves. Interest started to snowball. Jack Watson at the drugstore ordered fifty copies of the paperback edition of English translations, and they were sold out in two hours, even though everyone knows you don't get the full flavour of the poetry with a translation. Before long the school board had Delacroix giving night extension courses in French so people could get their Rimbaud in the original.

Once the courses got going, people talked of nothing else but Rimbaud's poems. You couldn't go into the British Arms without getting into an argument about the meaning of "Voyelles." For a while Baxter Martin and Clyde Dunbar weren't speaking to each other because Baxter followed the alchemical interpretation and Clyde believed the visual dimension was more important. People you met in the street would quote bits of *Une Saison en Enfer*, and you'd be expected to know what came next. But I guess "Le Bateau Ivre" was the favourite. Horace Warner, the United Church minister, wrote an article for the *Herald* to prove the St. Lawrence was one of the "fleuves impassibles," and after that we thought of it as "our" poem. Ms. Zanini's fourth-grade class chanted the whole thing at the school concert, and everybody said it was the highlight of the show.

The odd thing was, Rimbaud himself never took any interest in any of this. He knew what was going on, of course. When he came into the British Arms on Saturday afternoons, people would come over to his table and start firing questions at him.

Mostly they'd want him to explain a particular line or image. He was usually polite, but you could tell he found the whole thing pretty tedious. Finally, one Saturday, Steve Adams asked him if he would say, in a sentence or two, what the main thrust of his *oeuvre* was, and Rimbaud just got up and walked away without answering.

After that, he stopped coming in to drink. He'd do his shopping as quickly as possible and head straight home, not speaking to anyone he didn't have to. A few weeks later, matters came to a head. Young Dave Hutchinson, the high school kid who'd started the whole thing, stopped Rimbaud in the street and asked him to autograph a copy of the Penguin edition of the *Collected Poems*. Rimbaud said sure, he'd be happy to, as long as he didn't have to answer any questions. But as he handed the book back, he said, quite distinctly, "Listen, kid, I think you should know it's all a pile of shit." Several bystanders heard it.

That upset a lot of people. What sort of man would make a remark like that about great poetry? An interest in Rimbaud's biography blossomed overnight. New controversies erupted. There was the drug thing, for instance. Steve Adams said it was proof positive Rimbaud was a degenerate. But Clyde Dunbar said anybody could make a mistake (his son had received a suspended sentence for possession the year before), and anyway there was no evidence that Rimbaud still used drugs. Then there was the thing about his running guns for the Arabs. That put a few people off. But then somebody down at the Legion pointed out that it wasn't all that different from what Buzz

Beurling had done after the War. Rimbaud still had his defenders, but a lot of us were asking questions. And then there were mysteries. What about the "lost years," as we called them now, between 1891 and the day he arrived in our town, driving his Chevy pickup? How did he get into the country? And what was he doing out in Harry Graves's farmhouse, with all that chemistry equipment?

It was Baxter Martin's idea to invite him to be guest speaker at the next Rotary Club meeting. Baxter thought it would be a way of "clearing the air," as he put it. Everyone agreed it would be a good thing. When Rimbaud came into town the next Saturday, Baxter was waiting for him. "We used to think you were going to fit in here," Baxter told him. "Now we're not so sure." Rimbaud just stood silently while Baxter explained about the Rotary meeting, and how a lot of people thought Rimbaud had a funny attitude, and this would be a chance for him to explain himself. The poet thought it over for a minute or two and then said all right, he'd do it.

Everybody wanted to come. Joe Summers filled the banquet room at the British Arms with as many extra tables and chairs as he could get, and there were still people standing in the back. The atmosphere was tense. Not that anybody was expecting trouble, just that we knew the whole question of Rimbaud's status in our community was going to be settled once and for all, one way or the other. Baxter was the emcee, as usual. Wanting to be fair, he gave Rimbaud a big build-up: "a great poet, a man who needs no introduction…" and so on. Nobody really listened.

We were all staring at Rimbaud, who seemed completely at ease, even slightly bored. Then he was walking up to the microphone. There wasn't much applause.

We weren't prepared for the speech he gave. I guess we thought he'd give us some explanation as to why he'd been so indifferent to our interest in his poetry. Maybe he'd include some defence of his character regarding the drugs and the gun-running. Most of all, we wanted him to say that he hadn't meant it, when he'd said that his poetry was a pile of shit. But what we got was something quite different. He started by saying he understood we'd been puzzled by his behaviour, but that he wasn't going to try to justify it. Instead, he wanted to demonstrate his desire to be a good citizen. He paused to take a sip of water, and then announced that he was going to run as an independent candidate in the next federal election.

All over the room, people started talking. There was some laughter, but most of us saw immediately that the idea had merit. Our town is off in the corner of a large, mostly rural, constituency. We've never had an MP come from here. But once word got around that Rimbaud was world-famous, a great poet, and that electing him would focus national attention on our town, we knew he'd win easily. And once he was in, at last we'd have a Member of Parliament who'd be committed to doing something for us. Of course, we don't need that much. And we're not greedy. But an infusion of federal money would be nice. And maybe, we all thought, Rimbaud could finally do something about getting us our new bridge, through some federal-provincial cost-sharing program, or some cash grant for out-of-the-way areas—there must be plenty of ways to do things like that.

All these ideas were going through our minds in the two or three minutes it took Baxter to restore order. I guess Rimbaud's popularity had never been greater than it was at that moment. When he tried to speak again, he was stopped several times by cheering. Until people began to realize what he was saying. He'd begun to present his program, the policies he said he'd "work to have implemented." I can't remember much of it. Different people have different versions of what they heard him say.

I'm not very good on the details, and this all happened quite some time ago, so much of what he proposed would probably be irrelevant now. And just like with his poems, it seemed that everyone had two or three favourite specific points they wanted to talk about. Suffice it to say that life around here would be quite different if he'd been able to "implement" many of his ideas.

It was very quiet when he stopped speaking. There was no clapping but no boos or hisses, either. Audiences here are pretty well-behaved. True, two people at the back shouted "Communist!" and "Fascist!" simultaneously, but that was it. Still, everyone knew Rimbaud was through in this town. People started to leave, and Baxter didn't bother to go through the formality of thanking the speaker. Rimbaud, as I recall, went back to his chair and sat down, staring off into space as though completely unconscious of the effect he'd had.

Public opinion crystallized quickly. For the next two days, people talked about nothing else. That week's *Herald* had a front-page editorial about "undesirable elements in our midst" whose "weird philosophy conflicts with our hallowed traditions." There were several angry letters to the editor, too. But it was Horace Warner, in his Sunday sermon, who came up with the only practical idea, and we took it up, pretty much by consensus.

It was only a couple of weeks before Dominion Day. (I know they've given it a new name now, but we still like the old one.) Reverend Warner's idea was that the Boy Scouts should go around town collecting every volume of Rimbaud's poetry that hadn't already been thrown out. (We didn't have recycling back then.) On the first of July, they could bring the books down to Mackenzie King Park, by the river, where the fireworks display was to be held. As a kind of grand finale to the program, we could have a book-burning, the first in the town's history. Besides releasing a lot of pent-up emotion, Warner reasoned, that would also serve as a very pointed hint to Rimbaud himself about the town's new attitude toward him. The plan was immediately endorsed by the town council at a special meeting.

Dominion Day came, and everything went according to plan, but the book-burning turned out to be a bit of a flop. There just weren't enough books to make a very impressive pile, and a small bonfire is bound to be an anticlimax after a fireworks display. Maybe we should have had it earlier in the evening. Or maybe Warner's idea wasn't such a good one after all. When it was all over, some of us didn't feel like going home.

We sat on the riverbank, drinking straight rye out of paper cups. It was a hot night. We stared at the moonlit water, not saying much. (The river has a long name, hard for outsiders to pronounce—we hardly ever use it ourselves; to us, it's just "the river.") At first, nobody mentioned Rimbaud. He hadn't come into town since the day of the speech. Harry Graves had gone out to give him his month's notice. He said Rimbaud was outside working with his chemistry equipment, apparently dismantling it. They had a very short conversation. Rimbaud wouldn't say where he was going to go next. When Harry told him about the book-burning, he seemed surprised. "He acted like he didn't give a shit," Harry'd told us. We thought about this as we watched the water flowing toward the old covered bridge. Rimbaud had come here and made fools of us, and now he was getting ready to walk away. We didn't like it. It wasn't long before we ran out of rye.

I think it was Baxter Martin who finally made the suggestion out loud. It could've been Joe Summers. I don't think it matters. There were twelve of us. We took three cars. Crossing the bridge was like going through a dark tunnel, and we all felt that familiar shaky sensation, as if the whole structure was about to collapse, and then we were through, and driving maybe faster than we should have, along the two-mile stretch of road that led to the Graves farmhouse.

The funny thing was, Rimbaud was waiting for us, right at the gate. He must have heard the cars coming from a fair distance. Maybe he'd guessed who was coming and why. But then why didn't he try to get away in his truck? Or if he thought we might have cut him off, why didn't he make a run for it, across the fields? He had a fair chance to escape. Anyway, there he was.

It was so unexpected that when the headlights picked him up, I thought at first he was an animal that had strayed down from the hills. But that only lasted for a split second, and then I saw who it was. He was even smiling faintly. Cool as could be.

It didn't take long, and I guess the details aren't important. There was no record of anything that happened. In a town this size, it's not too difficult to keep things quiet, if everybody co-operates.

THE APOCALYPSE THEME PARK

'm a bit surprised when Melba suggests that we go to the apocalypse theme park on our first date.

"Melba," I say, "nobody goes *there* anymore, do they?"

"Of course they do," she says. "I was there myself only last week. There were tons of people. Multitudes."

Okay, I'm thinking. I'll play along. Actually I'm surprised that Melba would agree to go out with me at all. I don't know her that well. We've chatted two or three times in the laundry room in our building, and we've said hello in the elevator a few times, too. Today I help her carry groceries in from the parking lot.

When I put the bags down on her kitchen table, she turns and looks at me and says, "Harvey, what do you think of the Third World?"

I think carefully, sensing a possible turning point in our relationship. Which doesn't actually exist yet, of course. She's a cute little thing, if that doesn't sound condescending. (Wait a minute. I know, it does.)

But I haven't actually heard the phrase "Third World" for a long time. Is it out of fashion now? Hasn't it been replaced by "Global South" or something like that? How would I know?

But I'm dealing with a woman who goes to the apocalypse theme park, of all places. Maybe being deliberately old-fashioned. For obscure personal reasons, none of my business.

So I say that the Third World is okay by me. "It sure gets a rough time from cynical, power-hungry, exploitative Western governments and multinationals, though, doesn't it?"

She smiles in agreement. I feel reassured. But the apocalypse theme park? What an odd choice for a young woman like Melba. Nobody much our age goes out there these days. Older folks, maybe—but not as many of them as there used to be, either. And maybe a few younger people, but not like us. That may sound snotty, but I think there's a class thing here. I mean, here's Melba, a world-class research chemist (she's even discovered or invented her own molecules apparently), but guess where she wants to go?

She might as well be suggesting bowling or bingo.

Note to self: Remember to ask her whether you discover new molecules or invent them. Pretty impressive either way, I'm thinking.

Current speculation is that the main reason for the existence of the apocalypse theme park is to create some sort of collective sense of embarrassment, or to make us all feel bad generally. As far as contemporary scholarship can determine, that was probably the intent of the builders, way back when. I hypothesized it wouldn't be a good idea to raise this issue with Melba, though. And of course the park has come to mean something quite different to many people since then.

The truth is that when I ask Melba out, I'm kind of desperate for a date. I haven't been seeing anyone for about six months. That was when Melissa and I discovered that our relationship, like a cargo vessel of Panamanian registry, was foundering on the reef of irreconcilable differences. Such as her insistence that I abandon my career to start a new life with her in an ashram in Timmins.

"Abandon *what* career?" Melissa would ask. "Far as I can see, you just sit in your apartment all day, gazing into the void, and sometimes people send you cheques. What kind of career is that? And why couldn't they just send the cheques to Timmins?"

But that was six months ago. Melissa went into real estate instead of the ashram. Every once in a while I see her gliding around town in her new Porsche. She always waves and smiles when she sees me.

Melba wants to go out to the apocalypse theme park on a Tuesday afternoon, evidently a good time for her to get away from the lab. "Also, it won't be as crowded as on the weekend," she says. "Daddy always used to say that Tuesdays were the best days for going out there. I'm not sure why, but people seem to find it easier to have personal revelations on Tuesdays."

"I'm not looking to have any personal revelations," I say. "I wouldn't mind checking out the seven seals, though, and maybe the destruction of Babylon. I've always been kind of interested in those."

"No personal revelations?" Melba says, sounding really surprised. "I *always* try to have a personal revelation. And I definitely want to go to the lake of fire and the bottomless pit. I remember Daddy taking me to those places when I was little, and he said to me, 'Melba, here's all you need to know about the meaning of life.' Of course I had no idea what he was talking about then— but I sure do *now*."

I can hardly believe this, coming from a woman who's invented or discovered her own molecules.

We're having this conversation on Monday evening. She's come over to my place to drop off some books on the Third World, which, she has assured me, is still very much a thing, even if people don't use the phrase as much as they used to. "A rose by any other name," she says, a bit cryptically for me.

I ask her to explain and one thing leads to another, and she winds up spending the night. I'm pleased to find that a certain minor problem I've consulted my physician about appears to have solved itself.

When we meet in the parking lot next afternoon, Melba acts kind of shy. She's had to get up early to get to the lab, so we haven't talked at all in the morning.

"I hope you don't think I'm the kind of woman who does what we did last night," she says, blushing.

"Of course not," I say. "It never happened."

"What never happened?"

"Exactly."

We're starting to develop a really good rapport, I'm thinking. Melba is my kind of woman.

Soon we're hurtling down the expressway toward the apocalypse theme park, chattering away about the Third World. Actually, she does nearly all the talking. After a while I'm not really listening, just picking up the odd phrase here and there: "economic crisis… stolen heritage… pillage… deep structural adjustment… blaming the victim… sustainable alternative… "

Suddenly a familiar red Porsche zooms past us, honking.

"It's Melissa," I say aloud, despite myself. Then of course I have to explain.

"So, Melissa," Melba says, after I've finished what there is to say. She says it as if she's appraising a painting that's about to be auctioned off.

Don't you love it when women do this kind of thing? Do I care who her last boyfriend was? Or if she has one now, for that matter?

"Yep, that's Melissa," I say.

"Awfully big coincidence, her being out here, don't you think?" Melba is saying.

I agree.

By now we're getting pretty close to our destination. There hasn't been much traffic. In fact we've seen only about a dozen cars on the way out, including Melissa's Porsche.

"So," Melba is saying, "when Melissa wanted you to abandon your career and go to the ashram in Timmins, what career is it exactly that she wanted you to abandon? I mean, what do you actually *do* for a living, Harvey? I know it's none of my business, but."

She leaves the last sentence hanging. Would she like to *make* it her business?

Actually, it's rather difficult to explain what I do for a living. Somehow I've become adept at retrieving certain kinds of information that few people have access to, despite the fact that I don't need to leave my apartment to get it. It's all online of course, everything is online, but my particular skill lies in being able to find patterns in disparate pieces of information of a certain kind. I have clients who find some of this information very useful. I'm contractually obligated to keep my mouth shut about the whole business.

"What clients?" Melba asks me when I get this far.

"Oh, different ones. Government agencies. Corporations. My name gets passed on in certain circles."

"What kind of corporation?" Melba asks, her tone conveying just the slightest trace of frost.

"Well, all kinds."

"And are some of them the same sleazy multinationals hell-bent on ravaging the Third World and annihilating its innocent citizens?"

I sense that I'm losing ground here. The image of Melba as potential girlfriend is growing fainter by the second. She's waiting for an answer.

"Sleazy multinationals? Well, maybe some of them are. I wouldn't really know about that. But I just give them information.

I don't have anything to do with how they use it. I mean, it's just information, right? Objective. Neutral. I mean, it must be like you and your molecules, wouldn't you think? You've invented them or discovered them or whatever, but you can't control how other people use them, can you?"

We're just turning on to the access road to the theme park.

"My molecules," Melba says, "would never be party to the exploitation of the Third World. I'm not saying that other molecules wouldn't, but not mine. They'd disintegrate first."

After five minutes of silence, we pull into the vast parking lot, which is, predictably, almost empty. And I'm starting to feel there's something creepy about this place, sinister even. How can they be making money, whoever runs it? And who does run it? And what if their motive isn't to make money? What could it be? Now there's a scary thought.

Hoping to defuse the tension, I ask her which gate she wants to go through. (Of course there are twelve gates to the theme park.)

"Sapphire," she says. "I always go in through sapphire. In five minutes you can be staring into the bottomless pit."

We pass the amethyst gate, then jasper.

"It's around the next corner," Melba says. "I'll show you the parking space Daddy always used."

We turn the corner, and there's the sapphire gate, only one car parked anywhere near it, and wouldn't you know it's Melissa's Porsche?

Suddenly Melba brightens up, becomes all friendly again. "Harvey! Maybe you'll have a personal revelation today. Having to do, perhaps, with the sleazy way you earn your living. Maybe you'll be able to put it all behind you."

"Maybe I will."

"Harvey, I think that car is in Daddy's spot."

As we get closer, I can see that Melissa is looking in our direction, smiling benignly, as though she's been expecting us.

"Oh, it's not in Daddy's spot, it's in the spot right next to it— isn't that a coincidence?" There's no trace of irony in Melba's tone. She seems delighted, for some reason. "Oh, and Harvey?" she says, as I pull in beside the Porsche. She leans over and pokes my arm gently. "You know what never happened last night? I wouldn't mind if it didn't happen again."

Melissa is wearing earphones, bouncing around behind her wheel in time to music that we can't hear. She gives us a big wave, though.

"Me too," I say. "Or, I mean: not me either."

Melissa disengages the earphones and hops out expectantly.

I'm thinking there might be trouble, the two of them meeting like this. The truth is, I believe that Melissa is maybe still a bit interested in me, and she might be upset that I'm dating another woman. I'm concerned about the possibility of a minor altercation, an unseemly scuffle of some sort.

I introduce Melba by saying she has her own molecules and Melissa by saying she's in real estate.

"So we both have a strong interest in the physical universe," Melba says, sort of grinning politely at Melissa.

"I guess we do," says Melissa, grinning back.

I'm not quite sure what these grins mean. I try to conjure up one myself, but somehow it feels as though it doesn't quite work.

"So what do you think of Harvey?" Melissa asks, which I think is rather rude of her, although when Melissa does that kind of thing she can get away with it. She's *cute*, Melissa is. Cute can take you a long way, and Melissa is well aware of it. Of course Melba is cute too.

"Harvey? He's okay. I guess," Melba says, which I think is more understated than necessary. "Nothing's happened, though, has it, Harvey?"

"No, nothing," I say, trying another unsuccessful grin. "So what are you doing out here, Melissa?"

"Oh it's a regular Tuesday afternoon thing for me. This place always makes me feel better. It's sort of good clean fun, coming out here, I always think. Takes you back to an earlier time, when the air was pure, and the water didn't have that disgusting off-white foam on it all the time."

"What off-white foam?" I say. "I haven't noticed any—"

But Melba has drowned me out, saying, "We know who's responsible for *that*, don't we?"

We all stand there in the parking lot, contemplating this thought for a moment.

"So let's go in," Melba says then, throwing an arm around my shoulders, and the other around Melissa's, which I think is a bit strange, since they've only just met. Also Melissa is taller than Melba, so it's a bit awkward for Melba to reach up like that. But Melba seems to think it's the most natural thing in the world.

When we get inside, Melba is all for heading straight to the bottomless pit. I suggest we go for a sort of get-acquainted beer first, but Melissa says—oddly, I think—"Harvey, why don't *you* get a beer, while Melba and I just go on and check out the pit? We'll meet up with you later."

And before I can ask where or when, they just take off, arm in arm, whisking around the corner of one of the buildings near the entrance.

I think of running after them, but then I figure what's the point. Obviously Melba wants to ditch me for the time being. Maybe it's some kind of test.

So instead of following them, I just sort of stop and look around. You probably know how the apocalypse theme park is laid out. All the major attractions have separate buildings to themselves: the four horsemen, for example, the beast from the sea, the seven last plagues, the destruction of Babylon, the battle of Armageddon, the new heaven and the new earth. And many others, including, of course, Melba's faves, the lake of fire and the bottomless pit. And then of course, scattered throughout the park, there are various sideshows, concession booths, restaurants, bars. You can have your picture taken with a woman dressed like the Whore of Babylon, there's a compound where you can ride a pale horse exactly like the one ridden by Death, you can go to a booth where they'll give you a temporary mark of the Beast tattoo (or a permanent one, if that's what you're into), you can rent white robes if you want to impersonate the righteous, and so on.

I wander into a bar I choose at random and order a beer. For a few minutes I seem to be the only customer, but then I notice a tall, thin man with dark glasses sitting in the back corner. There's something familiar about him. He waves at me. "Harvey," he says. "Over here."

He speaks as though it's a command, rather than an invitation. I pick up my glass and make my way toward him. Who the hell is he?

"Siddown, Harvey, siddown. You think you don't know me, right? Just let me say this, Harvey." And now he utters a secret phrase, known only to myself and one other person.

At once I recognize my physician, Dr. Ashdod. I saw him only a couple of weeks ago because of a certain problem which now seems to have been solved. I had occasion to use this secret phrase during that appointment. Dr. Ashdod found it amusing; "naively euphemistic" was how he characterized it.

"Yes, Harvey, it's me. Surprised?"

I've been going to Dr. Ashdod since I was a kid. He must be well past retirement age by now. He's about a foot taller than I am, which makes him seem intimidating, no doubt unintentionally on his part. That plus the fact that he knows so much more about my body than I do. But I've always trusted his medical judgment. So am I surprised?

He doesn't wait for me to answer.

"You are surprised, aren't you? It's always a matter of surprise."

"What is?"

"Tuesday," Dr. Ashdod says with a smile that seems to me to be bordering on the sinister. The classic "sinister" smile. "Ever notice how lonely people can get on a Tuesday, Harvey?"

This idea seems so absurd that the only appropriate response I can think of is to agree.

"So you *have* noticed. Good for you, Harvey. I wouldn't have given you credit."

He smiles again. He has surprisingly good teeth, though his face is veined, spotted, ravaged in various repulsive ways. Is it possible that he looks worse than he did two weeks ago?

"Everybody lonely on a Tuesday," he says, taking a swig of his drink, a strange, medicinal-smelling liquid, yellowish-green in colour, that seems to have many ingredients. I know nothing, now that I think about it, about his personal life.

"Drink up, Harvey. My round next."

I sip my beer, not knowing what to say.

"I come out here every once in a while," Dr. Ashdod says, "always on a Tuesday. Is it nostalgia that draws us, Harvey? What do you think? Why does the apocalypse theme park embarrass us? Why do we prefer to pretend it doesn't exist, most of the time?"

I have no idea what he's talking about. "I'm out here on a date," I tell him.

"Ah yes, your new young woman. What is her name again? Selma? Melba?"

Did I mention Melba to him two weeks ago? I can't remember. It seems unlikely, though.

"How are you two getting on?"

"Nothing's happened," I say loyally. It's just possible that Melba is his patient, too—or maybe even related to him, for all I know.

"Of course not, nothing." He laughs, a hint of derision. "You young people." And then he repeats the secret phrase that I used to describe my physical problem. I think this is very unprofessional of him.

"Melba," he says reflectively. "Ever thought of what her name's an anagram of?"

I think for a minute. "Amble," I say confidently.

"That's the spirit, Harvey. Basically, you're a very healthy young man."

I'm about to point out that this appears to be a non sequitur, but he keeps going.

"And that other young woman you used to go out with, Melissa, wasn't it, think of what her name could turn into, assuming her middle initial is T, which I believe it is."

How could he have known that? Is Melissa his patient, too? He pauses now, as if to give me an opportunity to question him. I decide not to.

"Melba's a scientist, a research chemist. She's discovered or invented her own molecules."

"Sounds like a rock band from the fifties," Dr. Ashdod says. "Melba and the Molecules. One of Phil Spector's groups, no doubt. How droll." Dr. Ashdod permits himself a quiet chuckle. "Time to get serious now, though, Harvey."

"What do you mean?"

"Just tell me, Harvey. Where are we?"

I'm thinking I might as well play along.

"The apocalypse theme park."

"Near what major attraction?"

"Well, Melba said the bottomless pit was close by."

"No, Harvey," says Dr. Ashdod, removing his dark glasses, and fixing me with his icy stare, the dark eyes seeming, like his teeth, to belong to a much younger man, as though the decaying flesh was only a mask. "No, Harvey. This *is* the bottomless pit."

This declaration is accompanied by a really tacky echo effect, as in "pit-it-it-it-it."

I feel a jolt of terror but struggle to control myself.

"Shouldn't there be more elaborate special effects," I say, attempting to strike a conversational tone. "Maybe some of that smoky stuff they use at rock concerts?"

Dr. Ashdod smiles indulgently, in his glory now for sure. "Don't be a dickhead, Harvey. We don't need that stuff." He waves his arm ambiguously.

I look around the bar. Television cameras, apparently remote-controlled, glide toward our table from three directions.

"Smile, Harvey. We're on CCTV for the folks at the Bottomless Pit Theatre. Melba's cheering for you, Melissa's rooting for me. Of course the whole business will look quite different to them."

"What business?"

"Harvey, Harvey, Harvey. Get a clue. The 'business' is our conflict. Our conflict, Harvey. You versus me. Loser disappears into the bottomless pit forever. Half the audience will think you've won, half that I've won. And half of them will be right. Everything's fifty-fifty. That's reality."

"No, it isn't," I say with confidence. Where did I get it, this confidence? "That's not reality," I add, with a dash of contempt for good measure. "Reality!"

"Is there an echo in here, Harvey, or what? Yes, reality. The genius of the apocalypse theme park, Harvey, is that it functions as both illusion and truth simultaneously. What constitutes an afternoon's diversion for our charming friends in the other building is, for us, reality itself (-elf-elf-elf)."

I know there's no escape from this encounter, that if I try to leave I will somehow be prevented. Beneath the barroom floor, I know with certainty, the bottomless pit lies gaping. Yet I feel calm, still confident as I prepare to focus on the task at hand.

"Let's get started, Harvey. We're going to arm-wrestle. Too bad you won't be able to sell this information to your clients—it's a question of presenting it credibly, isn't it? There's simply no way. Let's shift our chairs a bit so that we get the right camera angles."

Numbly, I find myself doing as he says.

"By the way, Harvey, did I mention that I've got a thing going with Melissa now? I'm afraid she's been rather caustic about some of your, ah, idiosyncrasies." And here he adds the secret phrase that described the physical problem I used to have.

But such crude attempts to psych me out won't work. The situation has assumed a terrible purity that makes it easy for me to concentrate on what really matters.

We lock thumbs. "On the count of three," Dr. Ashdod says. I know he'll try to get the jump. I'm ready for him at two and a half, but he's stronger than I thought. He's got my forearm back at a forty-five-degree angle before I can do anything. Then we both settle in for the struggle to the finish.

And then one of three things happens.

1) I feel a strange power flowing through my arm. I start to push Dr. Ashdod's arm back up, and I know it'll be only a matter of time. It's Melba's molecules, I know instinctively, permeating every fibre of my arm, I can almost see them, tiny white radiant stones with Melba's name printed on them in neat utilitarian letters, and I can see that Dr. Ashdod knows that he's done for, and by the time our forearms are back to the position at which we started, I'm thinking, "When this is over, me and Melba, we'll take on the world together, no problem."

2) We enter an eternal moment of complete stasis. It comes to me that Dr. Ashdod has had a hard, sad existence—so much treachery, so many lies, so little that speaks of radiance and wholeness. Our hands disengage themselves, we stand up, we embrace, we weep together.

3) Inexorably, the old man's sinister strength wears me down, my forearm moves closer and closer to the pocked wooden surface of the table. I swear I can hear Melissa's scream of triumph mingled with the unmistakable sounds of weeping and gnashing of teeth, and I prepare as best I can for the endless plunge into the abyss.

SCAR

n the first place, I'm really bad with faces, I said. Really bad.

That's okay, said the one detective. We just want your honest take, that's all.

It was like on TV. There we were, in the room with the one-way glass. The suspects on the other side. Me and the two detectives and the defence lawyer on this. A nicely confined space. I felt safe.

Faces, I don't know, I said. Body types, I'm better on. Skin colour, a hundred per cent. And names. Never forget a name. Or a voice. But faces, sometimes a complete blank. Sometimes I'll be approached on the street by someone I think I've never seen before, and after we exchange a few words I'll remember the voice, and he'll be a close friend. Only then will the face make sense, after I've listened to the voice.

The defence lawyer was making notes. He was a big guy, six-four maybe, with shoulder-length grey hair. His name was Roy C. Batterton.

Close friends are forever playing practical jokes on me, I continued, revolving around this issue of recognition. I have a lot of close friends.

Let's just get on with it, shall we, said the first detective. His name was Jack Merkley. He wore cowboy boots. I didn't particularly like him. There was something duplicitous in the very core of his being, I theorized, and this deficiency manifested itself in subtle ways in his bearing, gestures, and intonation.

The other detective was called Patrick Daniel. He hovered in the background and said almost nothing. Once in a while he'd belch softly.

Someone began knocking on the door, in a rhythm and volume traditionally employed to convey urgency.

So far I had told the truth, and nothing but.

My wife sat hunched on a stool in the corner.

I wondered, idly, if I would be able to recognize her if I didn't know who she was to begin with. I've devoted many years of study to her face. But the lighting here wasn't that great.

I decided to play for time.

Aren't you going to answer it? I asked, referring to the knocking.

Go away! said Merkley loudly, to the door. This isn't a good time.

The knocking stopped for a moment, then picked up again.

Holy-o baldheaded.

Merkley seemed relieved. Let's check out that lineup, he said.

Five people standing there. They all looked pretty much the same to me. Five white males, probably in their twenties. I looked hard and long, but it didn't help.

Take your time.

Was it my imagination, or was there an edge of sarcasm in his voice?

It's the one in the middle, my wife said. He's the guy.

You weren't even there, I pointed out.

I'm sure it's him. He looks sneaky.

To me he looked no sneakier than the others. They all looked sneaky.

We know she's upset, Merkley said. We'll just ignore that. Between you and me, she's way off base.

Hey hey, cut that out, Batterton said. Any more coaching, and I'll pull the plug on this sucker.

Daniel cleared his throat and said, We're all in this together, Roy. You know that. When you come down to it, it's our kind against theirs.

I got a client to represent. Indigent and ignorant he may be, it's my sworn duty to do the best...

Put a cork in it, Roy, Merkley said forcefully. To me he said, Just focus on those faces. Any differentiating factors may be worth considering.

Five identical white males, all with that shifty look in the eyes that invariably implies up-to-no-goodness. One of them seemed to be snarling softly to himself, one smiled nervously, and the other three were completely impassive.

The pounding on the door started again, a different kind. Seemed like a battering ram. Fractured my concentration. What differentiating factor could there be?

It was getting dark, I said. I only saw him for a minute. Or less. Probably much less. And I *am* really bad with faces.

I had already decided not to tell them about the killing. Felt bad about it. Could be the man didn't know the Lord. Could be he went straight to hell. But I was justified. Man was trespassing. My property, broad daylight. As if he owned it and not me. What choice did I have?

Happened on the southeast lawn. Saw him from my study. Face pressed against the window, bold as brass. Chased after him with the John Deere. Cornered him down by the pine grove, where I had the ten-foot wall put in.

He knew what was coming. Stood there and faced me, as if daring me to do it. Didn't say a word. Totally inarticulate, no surprise there. Trespasser of the deepest dye. Looked him in the eye. Trespasser, I said. So he'd be in no doubt as to why. One shot was enough, well-placed as I made sure it was.

Tied him on the back of the John Deere and hauled him off to this secret place I know. Didn't want the servants to see him. Keep things simple. Buried him in the secret place. Case closed, I thought.

I forgive him now, as Scripture enjoins me to do. Forgive him his trespass. Hope he's with the Lord. But he had no business on the southeast lawn.

The battering noise stopped.

What do you want? Merkley shouted. There's a lineup going on in here.

A voice from the other side of the door. We're a concerned group of god-fearing citizens.

Daniel belched before he spoke. Lynch mob, he said. First one in months. I'll be damned.

What do you want?

We want that asshole you got in there.

I could tell by the body language of the other occupants of the room that I was the one being referred to.

He's busy selecting a criminal.

He's the criminal, said the voice. Murdered a trespasser only yesterday, down by the pine grove on his own southeast lawn. His servants got it all on video. We want justice.

Sorry about this, Merkley said to me. We don't know anything about that, he said to the voice.

Ask him, said the voice, where he was at 4:37 yesterday afternoon.

We got no probable cause. We're investigating something that happened at eight p.m. yesterday.

Walked right up the north drive and through a flowerbed, my wife said. True enough, I never saw him, but his footprints are all over the petunia bed. Tromped on a good many of them. Then he scared my husband half to death, staring in through the study window.

Go away and come back later, Merkley said to the door.

Or don't come back at all, Daniel said.

Murdered a trespasser, Batterton said pensively. I find that very interesting.

We're not going anywhere, said the voice. Oddly, I was unable to recognize it, despite my impressive track record in the voice department. Must be an outside agitator, I was thinking. Someone sent here to stir up trouble.

I could sense things slipping out of control. Let's pray about this, I suggested. The others had no choice but to comply, or pretend to. As I prayed, I saw the face of the trespasser I had killed, staring at me as he had the day before, standing by the pine grove on my perfect lawn. At least I saw a sort of generic face that *could* have been his. As I prayed, I explained to the Lord why I had acted as I had, and how I knew that He had blessed me by arranging for such a satisfactory result. After all, if the death of the trespasser had not been in His will, He could have made sure that the John Deere ran out of gas at a crucial point, or for my weapon to malfunction. But no, He had seen that my cause was just and had smiled down on me.

Amen, I said aloud. Let's wrap this up. I was sure that the Lord would continue to bless me now.

I stared at the five identical faces on the other side of the glass. Then I saw the differentiating factor. Thank you Lord, I thought.

It's the one on the far left, I said. The one with the scar.

For in truth it came back to me now that as I had been seated at my desk the previous afternoon studying the Scriptures, the face pushing against the glass of my study window, ghostly as it seemed at the time, or perhaps "dead white" is the convenient descriptive phrase, might as well have sported, if that is the word, might as well have sported a scar not unlike this one, jagged and meandering, like a cartographer's rendering of a major river, a river with many tributaries, seeking without success the release of union with the sea.

The one on the far left. I'm sure of it.

I could tell by the lawyer's disappointed snort that I had picked the right man.

Okay, we're done here, said Merkley.

It was strangely quiet for a moment, but then we became aware of various small noises emanating from the general area of the keyhole.

Somebody picking the damn lock, Daniel said. God-fearing lynch mob, most likely.

Might as well open it for them, said Merkley. They're bound to do it themselves anyway.

Daniel swung the door open with a theatrical flourish, as if inviting an audience to applaud. A tall man was kneeling in the open doorway, hands filthy with lock-picking equipment. Like so many people, he looked vaguely familiar.

It's Robert McMichael, my wife hissed, sensing my puzzlement.

My best friend. Of course. I knew him now. My best friend, but a man with whom I had recently quarrelled over a point of doctrine having to do with the issue of the premillennial rapture.

We got the body, McMichael said. A crush of ne'er-do-wells filled the corridor behind him.

I was taken aback, not so much by the revelation that McMichael was leading the mob as by the realization that somehow this dim-witted person had become my best friend. Imagine actually believing in something as loony as the premillennial rapture!

Found it in the asshole's secret hiding place, McMichael continued. Turned out not to be so damn secret after all. A body, he repeated. How's that for probable cause? Good enough for us, ain't it, boys?

Affirmative grunts from the layabouts behind him.

Hang on now, Merkley said. We got to follow procedure here. We'll look into it, same as we would any other report of a trespasser's body found in somebody's secret hiding place.

Daniel belched loudly, a gesture I interpreted as supportive.

I confess to being somewhat intimidated. How had the rabble been allowed to get into the police station? Obviously through confederates on the force. Possibly Jack Merkley and Patrick Daniel were my last best hope for justice to prevail. I have already mentioned my earlier intuition about Merkley's character. By now I had a strong conviction that both men were hopeless reprobates, willing hosts to the worm of sinfulness even now doubtlessly gnawing through the metaphorical vitals of their respective souls.

Nonetheless I got behind Merkley, made sure he stood between me and McMichael.

Meanwhile my wife had begun to whimper, her perennial weakness of character beginning to reveal itself.

Let's all keep calm, said the lawyer. Everything's under control.

Easy for you to say, I thought. You with your pretentious shoulder-length grey hair. And equally pretentious middle initial. Roy C. Batterton my ass.

I backed into the glass and turned around.

The men on the other side were shuffling around in confusion, waiting to be told what to do, as you would expect of people who could credibly be identified as trespassers.

My eye was drawn inexorably to the one on the left, standing still now, apart from the others, to the scar, to the point on the skin at which the blood-redness began to well up from oblivion, *fons et origo* of our present condition.

I began to pray, again.

APPRENTICE

That was years ago now, many years, decades even. Don't even think about it unless somebody asks, which doesn't happen often. It's a different life now, completely different. Like this morning, I wake up, it's the woman, she's shaking me. "Good morning, turdface!" she says, big grin, ear to ear. "Wha?" I say. "Rise and shine, she's daylight in the swamp. Get your ass in gear, numbnuts, you're gonna be late." And she's right, the woman, she's always right. But I don't mind, not at all. I'm never really late. Of course it's only a job, as they say, nothing special—sweat of the brow, salt of the earth, penny saved, poor get poorer, you know what I'm saying. But I don't mind, somehow.

But taxidermy, you want to hear about taxidermy, you want to hear about my master, the *arch*-taxidermist he became, years later. You want to hear about "the lost years" (in quotation marks), you want to know what he was like *before* he made it to the big time. Right? Am I right about that? You're like the people who want to know the real facts about Atlantis or what Jesus was doing before he hit thirty. Beside the point, if you ask me. Barking up the wrong tree.

But I'll tell you anyway. No problem. As you know, my master was freelancing then, had his own set-up in the vast forests of the north. That's what they say in all the biographies, right, "the vast forests of the north"—hundreds of kilometres from anywhere, total seclusion. Well, not exactly. There were other people living there, societies that had been there for thousands of years, but in those days they somehow didn't really count. From our perspective. Yes, we referred to them as "natives." As in, the natives are restless. Well, we don't say that anymore, do we? Moved on, haven't we? Haven't we? Contrary to what you might have heard, my master always treated them with respect. Of course we depended on them to get our specimens for us. And what specimens we got! What a variety of species! One of the reasons, he once told me, that he'd set up shop in the middle of nowhere was that he could perfect his techniques in secrecy. Secrecy, he said. To develop trade secrets. Although it wasn't really a trade. It was much more than that. To him, at least.

I know there's been controversy about exactly what specimens we had during those years. I don't pretend to be able to settle all the disputes, especially the ones involving animals that can't be proven ever to have existed. But I can confirm this. We did have the Arctic iguana, the medieval armadillo, Hammurabi's sloth, the oriental vice-marmot (how it got there nobody knows), the Aristotelian salamander, among others, many others.

My master was a short man, white hair even then, skin very pale, meticulously clean-shaven, something austere and antiseptic about him. Son of a barber, that part of the legend is true. Apart from that, I knew almost nothing about his personal life before I met him. He wore glasses even though he didn't need to. A fashion statement? But there was no one to hear it. Except me, of course, and I'm pretty sure I wouldn't have counted.

There was something unsettling about his eyes, as though he was concealing something, maybe without being aware of it himself. But he probably was concealing something, and he probably was aware of it. "Eyes characterized by a willed opacity," that's what I wrote in my journal at the time. Oh I know I don't talk like that now. I don't even know what that *means* now, "willed opacity," shit like that. Pretentious. Different strokes, right? And I *am* different now. Then I was dedicated. Taxidermy was my life.

But enough about me. You want to know more about him, about the taxidermist, excuse me, *arch*-taxidermist as he is now, not me. "Precision above all else," he'd say. And once he said to me, "Kid, there's two important things in this world, flora and fauna. Flora we can trample underfoot, we can hack her down, we can shred her into little bits. That's what she's there for. But fauna. Fauna, now. That's a different matter. Fauna is raw material for us to ennoble by means of the sacred science of taxidermy. Fauna we can elevate to the realm of the categorical imperative." (Okay, maybe he didn't say "categorical imperative," I didn't write that one down in my notebook, but it was some phrase like that.)

And one other personal thing you might be interested in, they all are. Everybody wants to hear about this one. One day, out of the blue—we were working on a bird, I remember, possibly Heisenberg's swallow—he said to me, "At one point in my life I had to decide whether I was going to do nothing from then on but listen to Charlie Parker's music, or do something else. I decided to do something else." He wouldn't elaborate, despite my subtle reminders that I'd be a sympathetic listener. And I remember he worked very late that night, poring over his charts and graphs, oblivious to my comings and goings. (Normally he retired as early as nine o'clock.)

And one other incident you might want to hear about. One day the local people inadvertently killed a god, the only time this ever happened while I was there. I've forgotten which god it was, there were so many of them I don't think they had names for every last one. But a god for sure, all the infallible marks were there. The local people were terrified. What calamity might now befall their community? They must have thought that by bringing the carcass to my master, the mysterious outsider who would trade with them for dead animals, perhaps they could avert the disaster they all foresaw. My master, they must have thought, perhaps had access to some mysterious source of power that could be used for their benefit. Considering his interest in exotic dead animals, they realized that presenting him with this most exotic dead animal of all might make him inclined to do what needed to be done to ensure their survival.

So they carried the body into our workroom and placed it on the slab.

My master seemed very subdued. He signalled to me that I should pay the men who had brought the body to us double the usual rate for rare beasts of that size, the size of an average human male. When I'd done that, and the natives had left, he told me to lock the door, and then to come over to assist him. From somewhere he produced a tray full of delicate-looking silver instruments. Familiar though I was with his equipment, I'd never seen them before. "The body of a god," he whispered. And then looked directly at me. And I saw that his eyes were no longer opaque. I saw something there that I wasn't supposed to see. It lasted for only an instant, but for that instant it was as though I was someone else somewhere else, someone seeing something that no one had seen before, ever.

What was the guy's name? A long one. Oppenheimer, that's it! That's who I was. Oppenheimer at Alamogordo. Then it was over and he got down to work.

That's all I can tell you. I was another person back then. Dedicated, the way he was, in my own small way. Now it's different—day's work for a day's pay, sweat of the earth, salt of the brow, home in the evening, home from the hill, home where the heart is. You know what I'm saying, right?

And the woman of course, always the woman. See that? See that there? She did that, left hook out of nowhere, didn't mean to, did it playfully. Playfully! Doesn't know her own strength. Does fifty chin-ups a day, runs half-marathons, no harm in her. Really. "Shouldn't have let your guard down, sucker," she told me. And gave me the big grin, ear to ear, a handful she is, several, more than I can handle. A killer, that woman. She'll be the death of me yet.

GARABANDAL

Father Vincent arrives unannounced, as usual. Father Vincent is really my Uncle Bob, but when he became a priest he took the other name. He writes his signature on Christmas and birthday cards as "Father Vincent (Bob)."

Anyway, he shows up at the front door, it's about four-thirty in the afternoon, Saturday. I knew he was back in Ottawa, of course, his annual visit to the hometown. He spends most of his time with my mother and the aunts, especially Kathleen, the alcoholic. Every year she sobers up for him, so he likes to pass some time watching her not drink.

He says, "God bless you, Ray," and I ask him in. He has this funny way of saying "God" out of the side of his mouth so it sounds like "Gawd." Maybe he thinks it's more reverential or something, to say it that way. Or maybe because he's a priest he thinks he should have the right to pronounce it his own way. He probably doesn't even know he does it, but you can't help but notice.

Christine comes in and I can see she's pissed off thinking maybe he's going to stay for dinner and she hasn't got the time to do anything special. But then he says he can't stay, he's only come to bless the house.

I feel like saying who asked him to come and bless the goddamn house, but I don't. I get Chris to call the kids in from the backyard, because that's the kind of thing he'll get off on, blessing the house while the kids watch.

While she's out of the room, he asks me if she's going to church with me yet and I say no, and I think now he's probably going to ask whether *I* go, and so to change the subject I ask him about Garabandal. He's very big on the Garabandal thing. A couple of years ago he brought a film, the Garabandal kids running up and down a hill when they were supposed to be having a vision of the Virgin Mary. But you couldn't see the Virgin Mary, just the kids. Anyway, he got in on the ground floor of Garabandal. He's expecting something pretty big in the near future, though he won't say exactly what.

So I ask him if there's anything new on the Garabandal front, and he says no. But this group in the States has chartered a plane on standby or something for the next visitation, and they've reserved a seat for him. Somebody's paying for it, a rich couple from New Orleans.

By this time Patrick and Michelle have come in. They don't really remember him from last year. I can see they're both a little scared, especially Patrick.

Then he says, "You don't have any holy water, do you, Ray?" I don't say anything for a minute and then he says, "No, I guess you wouldn't." I feel like telling him I've got a case in the basement, but he wouldn't appreciate the humour. He likes to say that he's got a sense of humour and doesn't mind people poking fun at him (that's his phrase, "poking fun"), but no one should poke fun at the Church. You can hear the capital C in Church when he says it. Anyway, he says it doesn't really matter, he'll just bless the ordinary water, and Chris goes and gets it for him.

Then he starts walking through the house, sprinkling water, and I can see the kids think it's great, an adult throwing water around like that. Patrick is jumping up and down, and Father Vincent is going, "In the Name of the Father and of the Son and of the Holy Ghost," and Michelle is saying to Christine, "What's he *do*-ing, Mummy?" the way kids do. And Chris says to me, "You explain it, you're the Catholic." I say, "Wait till he's gone."

Meanwhile Father Vincent gets to the basement stairs and says, "I think I can get the basement from up here, Ray," and gives it a few long-range sprinkles. I guess he's on a pretty tight schedule.

Then he asks about my dad, the way he always does. Since my parents split up, Vincent's had no reason to see him, my dad being the unconverted pagan Protestant. So what am I supposed to say? The last time I saw the old man, he said, "Geez, you know I may be gettin' older, but I still wake up in the morning with a semi on." Chris was there too, he said it right in front of her. That's my dad—real class. So I say to Vincent that he's doing okay. I don't mention the girlfriends.

Vincent says it's too bad about him and Mum, like he always does. "It's too bad Hal never became a Catholic," he says, and then in the same breath he asks if the kids are going to Catholic schools, and I say they are and when I ask, he says that nothing's happened lately, Garabandal-wise. But he takes it so seriously I don't think he even realizes I'm sticking it in.

The whole Garabandal thing is more complicated than you might think. It's not just between the kids and the Blessed Virgin. The Americans have taken over somehow. There's some guy named Joey in Brooklyn who blinded himself while repairing a car when he was a teenager. (I swear I'm not making this up.) Anyway, Joey had a vision about Garabandal after he was blinded, and part of the revelation was that the whole business, whatever it is, is going to happen before he dies. Now Joey's into his forties, I think, so it's not as though he's got forever. So I ask Vincent how Joey's doing, is he in good shape, and so Vincent says, really serious, "Yes, he's thinking of moving to Spain so that he'll be there for the big moment." I ask him what's going to happen then, and Vincent says then we'll all see ourselves as we really are, and the whole world will turn to God. That's how he put it. I'm not denying it's a nice idea.

So Vincent says goodbye and Gawd bless you a few times, and drives off into the sunset, except that it isn't the sunset yet, and I go back in to explain to the kids what he was doing.

Later I hear Michelle telling her friend from across the street that there was a man here today doing something to protect us from God.

Then Mum phones and asks was it a nice visit and I say yes. And she says he's over counselling Kathleen, that's how she puts it, and how next week he's going to be leading a retreat for nuns in Cincinnati. He's based in Kansas now, but he travels a lot. That's his big thing now, retreats for nuns.

• • •

My father has large ceramic squirrels on the roof of his house, a mother and three little ones. In his bedroom he's got a wooden mobile of a Canada goose. If you pull a string, the wings flap.

Once on a trip to California, on official government business, he drove back fifty miles, with three impatient colleagues in the car, to the restaurant they'd had lunch in—so that he could buy a fish made out of gilt seashells, drinking out of a cocktail glass. "I knew I'd never see another one like it," he says. The fish is grinning. You can see it mounted on his living room wall.

He's been to Atlanta, Georgia, twice and still calls it "Atlantic."

I could go on. My daughter Michelle, who's seven now, doesn't like the way he kisses her. He sucks on her cheek, somehow, and she always tries to get away. He did the same thing to Jackie, my sister-in-law, at her wedding. She didn't complain about it then, but now she'd tell him to fuck off.

At the time when he started the divorce proceedings, he said,

"I need somebody I can feel close to, somebody I can read *Reader's Digest* with."

He was born out of wedlock, as he likes to put it. Only recently he discovered that his biological father was a Jewish Mountie. Is it only in my family that these things happen? When we talk on the phone, he usually starts by saying, "This is Corporal Cohen speaking," and he ends the conversation with "Well, I guess I'll be seeing you at the goddamn synagogue. Shalom."

The Sunday morning after Father Vincent's visit, he calls me early, wanting to meet at a restaurant for breakfast. "Not Christine and the kids," he says. "Just you. It's really important."

We meet at a place in a small plaza in Nepean, not far from where his number one girlfriend lives. He's sitting near the back, wearing dark glasses, a Blue Jays cap, and the sweatshirt with his name on it—his full name and nothing else—that I gave to him as a joke for his birthday two years ago. He didn't get it.

"Ray, over here," he says, even though I've been looking right at him from the moment I got in the door.

He calls to a waitress. "Honey, get my son a cup of coffee, will you?" People are turning to look now.

The young server is bright-looking, probably a university student. I can tell she's struggling to keep her expression neutral as she turns to get the coffee.

"I come in here all the time now," my father says. "It's like family."

"That's nice," I say. We don't say anything for a minute. The server comes back with my coffee. I'm on time, but he's already had his breakfast.

"This little girl here is the best waitress west of the Pecos. This is my son, Ray. A big shot in the government, makes even more than I do. Ray, this is, this is—geez, I'm sorry, honey, I've forgotten your name."

She has a name tag that says "Tiffany" on it. She points to it, smiling mock-sweetly.

"Yeah, but that might be an alias," my father says, never at a loss.

I roll my eyes to show I've got nothing to do with this, but I can tell she's decided I'm the enemy too. She's got a bit of a problem with her complexion, I can see now—there's a lot of makeup.

"Might be an alias," my father says again, laughing at his joke. I tell her I'll have the number three with orange juice and eggs over easy. She nods and goes away without saying anything.

"Whaddya think of those?" he says, gesturing.

Then we get down to it. He wants information about Mum, as usual. She refuses to speak with him directly, even has an unlisted number now. What he wants to know is what the lowest figure is that he could get away with for a final settlement in the divorce. This has been dragging on for years now, it seems.

"The way I figure it," he says, "both our lawyers spent last winter in Florida tanning their goddamn bums, spending our money. That doesn't make sense."

What really doesn't make sense is that he's the one who's mostly responsible for this, fighting every inch of the way, refusing even to make routine maintenance payments, so that Mum's lawyer has to drag him into court every month. It's occurred to me that he enjoys the battle, that he doesn't want this last link to her to be cut off. There's no point in telling him this, though.

Tiffany comes back with my food. Dad pays no attention to her this time—he's busy making calculations on his napkin, trying to justify his ridiculous low offer.

"Tell her I'm serious about this," he says. "I want to wrap this thing up. By the way, I know she's making a few bucks babysitting. I've got spies."

I explain patiently that I can't reveal anything. I have to stay neutral.

"I know. You're a good kid. But can you not give me just a *rough* estimate of what she makes in an average month?"

When I'm finished, Tiffany comes over with the cheque. It lies balanced against a waterglass in the middle of the table. Dad makes small talk until I pick it up.

"What'd she write on the back?"

"Have a nice day, Tiffany."

"That's what she always writes." He looks disappointed. "I thought she was giving you her phone number, that's why I didn't pick it up."

My father pauses. You can see the lightbulb flashing on. "Ever fool around on Christine at all?"

• • •

That afternoon the Johansens come by, uninvited. We haven't seen them for two years, since they moved to Toronto. They used to live right across the street. Johansen is one of these really sarcastic guys, always looking for a laugh at somebody else's expense. I remember once he really pissed me off. I was digging the foundation for the family room I built on to the back of the house, something he could never do in a million years. So there was a big pile of dirt in the backyard where the deck is now. "Reminds me of *Close Encounters of the Third Kind*," he said. "Ever see it?" I told him I had, but he wanted me to just shut up and wait for his stupid punchline. "Ever think you might be like the guy in that movie, maybe unconsciously obeying the commands of some alien intelligence?" The way he said it, you knew he thought I was really stupid to put all that energy into building something.

He's doing well now in Toronto, he tells me, hinting that his salary is about $50k more than he thinks mine is. He's an engineer. His field is remote sensing. A really hot ticket just now, he says, and will be for the foreseeable future. And you can tell he thinks he can see farther into that future than you can.

We're sitting on the deck, drinking a beer. Denise, his wife, is inside with Christine. Christine wants to show her how we've redone the living room. They're up for the weekend, visiting her folks, he says, and they thought they'd drop by the old neighbourhood. See how our old friends are getting along—but there's an edge to his voice meaning that we're not really their friends anymore. Probably Denise insisted on this visit, I'm thinking.

"How's old Frank," he says, meaning Frank McCafferty, our next-door neighbour. And he starts to imitate Frank's voice, kind of soft-spoken and confused. Frank's the classic henpecked husband, afraid to go to the store without Delores's permission. Devout Catholic, always careful to say "sugar" instead of "shit." Then there's "fudge" or even "double fudge." It's easy enough to make fun of a guy like that.

Frank spent some time in the Royal Ottawa last winter. I went to visit him, and he told me his life just didn't seem to mean anything anymore.

Okay, I thought, I'll give it a shot. Frank, I said, you're only sixty-seven, your kids are married and doing well, you've got a good pension, you've got your health, and so does Delores. You could travel, or just relax and enjoy life. Golf in summer, curling in winter, whatever you want. It felt weird saying this to someone thirty years older. At a certain point I saw that he was crying. He didn't say a word, but there were tears streaming down his face.

When he came back home, he never mentioned my visit. He seems fine now.

Johansen realizes that his Frank imitation isn't going over well, so he starts talking about the Barnards, the Mormon family that lives next to their old place. The only Mormons either of us has ever met in person, except for the young guys in the black suits that come to your door. The Barnards: not at all representatives of the idyllic family life that Mormon propaganda would have you believe is standard—six kids, all of them murderous. Darrell Barnard is a lawyer for some government department. A weird guy—ripped his lawn up and had the yard AstroTurfed so he wouldn't have to take care of it. Spends a lot of time shooting baskets in his driveway, but if you stop to watch him for five minutes, you see that he's terrible, can't sink one shot in ten.

"What got me," Johansen is saying, "is the way they were always going off to meetings or whatever, the whole family in that van, packed like sardines. Those Mormons—it must be like China used to be, everybody pretending everything is wonderful all the time. Drinking their fruit juice or whatever."

He's waving his empty glass to show me he wants another beer. I get up to get it as Michelle comes out onto the deck and spots the bowl of potato chips on the table. She asks me if she can have some, and I say yes, but when she reaches for them, Johansen jumps out of his chair and blocks the bowl with his arm. Michelle backs off a bit and looks at me. Before I can say anything, Johansen says, "It's all right, go ahead, it's only a joke." But then he does the same thing again. Michelle can't quite decide if this is funny. For an instant she looks as though she's going to cry. Then she tries again and Johansen blocks her off again. Michelle tosses her head, the same gesture Christine would make, and marches back inside, not looking at me. Johansen is grinning. I feel like plowing him in the mouth.

A bit later Chris and Denise come out to join us. After two minutes of awkward conversation, the phone rings and I go inside to answer it, glad to get away. It's Father Vincent (Bob). "Ray," he says, "listen to this."

There's a long pause. I think maybe he's got a tape of the Blessed Virgin speaking at Garabandal, but what comes over the phone is music, big band stuff, "String of Pearls," Glenn

Miller. He plays the whole thing while I wonder what the hell is going on.

"Ray," he says when it's over. "I think that's particularly fine music, don't you?"

"Yes. Very fine."

"That's what I thought. Takes me back. I was just playing it for Rosemary here and I thought you'd enjoy it too. Rosemary, do you want to speak to your son? No, she doesn't, Ray. Gawd bless you." And he hangs up. When I go back out onto the deck, Christine and the Johansens are talking about the time that a Barnard two-year-old wandered out onto the street one stormy January afternoon, wearing only his, or her, underpants. Another neighbourhood legend.

And of course a few minutes later the phone rings yet again. This time it's my father, wanting to know if I've passed his offer on to Mum yet. I explain about Father Vincent being in town, something I hadn't mentioned at the restaurant.

"That asshole," he says. "Better wait till he's gone back to his goddamn monastery. Tell him I'm sticking with the Chosen People. Tell him Corporal Cohen always gets his mick. Scare him back over the border. Shalom."

I don't go back out to the deck, where Christine and Denise are engaged in an intense conversation about, as far as I can gather from fifteen seconds of eavesdropping, nothing, nothing at all (amazing how women can do that). Instead I wander into the TV room, thinking I'll check on the ball game or maybe watch a few minutes of a golf tournament, hoping that by the time I've done that, the Johansens will be ready to leave. I turn the TV on and sit down. And of course I fall asleep.

And I dream. I dream I'm building something in the backyard. It's made of wood and it's already quite high, well above the level of the roofs of the neighbourhood bungalows. It's hard to say exactly what it is. Maybe something like a lighthouse. I've never been inside a lighthouse. I've built a spiral staircase to the top. I'm about halfway up, where I've built a sort of playroom for Michelle, a treehouse kind of thing where she'll keep her favourite stuffed animals and other treasures. I ask her if she wants to come to the top, but she says she's happy where she is, so I go up the stairs by myself. I'm carrying a boom box. It's playing Father Vincent's music, Glenn Miller's greatest hits or something—"American Patrol," "In the Mood," all of them.

When I get to the top I look down at the whole neighbour-hood. It's almost like being in a plane. But there's nothing happening down there, the whole place seems dead. Except that I can see Christine down in the yard holding Patrick in her arms, and they're both looking up at me. And I'm calling down to them to come on up, but as I'm speaking the words I realize that I don't recognize the sounds, as though I'm automatically translating everything into a language that nobody understands.

BROTHER

take the ferry to Victoria on a Wednesday morning, in my
rented car, carefully chosen to not be too ostentatious. It would
make more sense for me to fly across. And to stay in a hotel, for
that matter, instead of on my brother's couch. But that would
send the wrong message, as they say. I try to be careful, visiting
my brother and his family.

It's May, bright but colder than it should be. The ubiquitous
tourists are out on deck, though, wearing heavy sweaters, gear-
ing up to take pictures of the Gulf Islands. I stay inside with my
laptop, reading the Investing section of the *Globe*. Poetry of the
names: Canadian Pacific, Emera, Fortis, Keyera, Kinross, Nutrien,
Telus, Algonquin, Pembina, and so on. It's endless. Once I was
going to be a poet. But now I'm wishing I could strike up a conversation with someone who could find the poem in that list.

I'm not looking forward to this, my brother and his family. It's been two years. But I had to come to Vancouver, business, and my mother, our mother, made me promise to "look in on" Scott and Renee. She meant, spy on them, look for the telltale signs of dry rot in the marriage, signs of desperation, evidence that my brother, my brilliant brother, had failed once and for all.

But Renee sounded welcoming on the phone last night, even expressed disappointment that I could stay only twenty-four hours. Important dinner meeting Thursday evening, I explained, not quite telling the truth.

"You businessmen are such assholes," she said, cheerfully. Renee comes from salt-of-the-earth NDP stock. If lawyers and MBAS could be expelled from the planet, she thinks, the millennium would begin. After a decade, she still seems not to know what to make of me as a brother-in-law.

There's a mild sense of being let down when the ferry finally arrives at Swartz Bay, end of the artificial otherworld of the journey, me and the Investing section of the *Globe*. The real world awaits. Driving through the pastoral landscape toward the city, I let everybody pass me.

My brother's house is about a kilometre or so from the ocean, on the Saanich side of Oak Bay. A small house, for a family of four. It's about eleven-thirty when I get there. Scott's the only one home. There's always something grudging about the attention he gives me, I think, as we shake hands. Friendly, but distantly friendly, and grudging. Irony in the handshake, it's an old game, but at the same time I'm distracting him from serious matters.

He's three years older and always will be, though forty-one and thirty-eight don't seem all that different.

We both say something noncommittal, as we judge each other again. He looks relaxed, even smiles as he asks me if I want coffee. Is it possible he's actually enjoying his life? And then I catch something in his eyes and wonder if, under certain circumstances, my brother might ever be capable of murder.

We walk through the small living room, with its overflowing bookshelves, the TV they've had since before they were married, the incongruous reproduction of a Hieronymous Bosch triptych over the couch where I'll sleep tonight. Bosch in the living room, pathetic stab at unconventionality. That's my bro. There are toys everywhere.

"It's a Fisher-Price minefield in here," I say, first attempt at humour. No response at all, not even an eyeblink, beneath contempt. The ball still in my court.

"Where is everybody?"

"Renee teaches Grade One. Her salary is what keeps the family afloat. Geoffrey goes to daycare. Sarah's at her school."

The refrigerator is plastered with drawings the kids have done. Scott starts to brew the coffee. I feel an urge to leave. We have nothing to say to each other. We're both still alive, we're the same people as last time, more or less. That about covers it.

"I'll go and get some beer for later."

"We've got some."

"We'll need more. It's okay, I'll get it while the coffee's getting ready."

He gives me directions slowly, as though he were talking to one of his kids.

Scott has a PhD in Philosophy. He hasn't worked in two years. Before that he taught as a sessional lecturer at several universities, a year here, two years there. Victoria was the end of the line—part-time instructor in the Education Faculty. A permanent academic job seems out of the question now. He's had his chances, he's been published extensively, he's again and again been shortlisted for tenure-track jobs. But he's bad at interviews—too reticent, not enthusiastic enough. He's kept at the writing, though. He's almost finished a book he's been working on for years.

When I come back with the beer, he says, "Do you still jog? Excuse me. Run?"

"Yeah." I run a lot, several days a week, but I don't tell him this.

"Let's go when we've finished the coffee. I've got extra shoes and stuff."

"How far?"

He shrugs. Part of the game—he won't reveal the exact nature of the challenge. Old rituals. But then, instead of delivering an evasive answer, he says, "What does she want, blood?" Meaning our mother. "Does she want you to go back east with a bucketful of my blood? A pound of my flesh?"

When we're ready, we change into shorts and T-shirts, and head out. It's warmer, now, with the noontime sun. Scott leads me toward the ocean, through Oak Bay. There's no direct route. He's going slowly. And he's thin, I'm thinking, My goodness, he's thin! As in, thin as he was at sixteen or eighteen. Can this be good? No, it can't. Whatever it is, he's doing it to himself. For his own inscrutable reasons. When we get to the street running parallel to the beach, we turn around. I increase the pace slightly. He keeps up for a couple of blocks. I start going a bit faster. Now I know I'm in better shape than he is; he's starting to suck air. Two blocks from home he gives up and decides to walk. I'm sitting on the front steps when he comes back. We don't say anything.

Of the whole family, Sarah is the one who's happiest to see me. She's nine. I'm her only uncle, and she loves me on principle despite my habit of showing up for brief visits every couple of years. She throws her arms around me and starts listing the things we have to do, baseball and Monopoly first. She wants to show me what she's learned in her gymnastics class, a special one downtown that she goes to after school two days a week. She's a white in swimming, she says, the highest level. After she's finished white, she'll do diving. She drags me off to play catch in the backyard.

"So," Renee is saying later, "how is the old bitch doing?" I'm shocked, a bit. Two years ago she wouldn't have said this. She's bitter that it's been only her parents who've helped with the mortgage. After Dad died, Mum insisted that Scott should "stand on his own two feet," as she puts it. "The way Eric has," I'm sure she would add, referring to me. And of course Scott refuses to let me help financially. "Matter of principle," he'll say. Case closed.

"She's doing all right," I say. "I don't see her that often. But she phones a lot. She's okay."

It's just the two of us in the kitchen drinking beer. Scott has had to drive Sarah to gymnastics, four-thirty to five-thirty. He'll probably hang out in bookstores downtown until it's time to bring her back. Renee is looking out the window, keeping an eye on Geoffrey in the backyard.

"Okay," she echoes sarcastically. "And why shouldn't she be? *She's* okay. And *you're* okay."

This is her third beer. She knows I've offered Scott money, knows he won't accept anything. His problem, not mine. Her problem. Don't take it out on me, lady.

But then she turns toward me and smiles, a bit blearily, and pats my knee and says, "That's okay, Eric. It's not your fault if you're rich."

She's put on some weight, Renee has, a fair bit in two years. Scott is thinner than he's ever been. She gets drunk easily. He can drink all night and get more sober than he is usually, if that were possible. A true marriage of opposites. But she wasn't this bitter two years ago, when she had the same reason to be. She's waiting for me to make the ritual gesture of offering her cash, which I know will be rejected on the grounds that Scott would somehow find out. Matter of principle. Scott's principle.

I haven't been listening.

"Last time we took the ferry over," Renee is saying, "there was this really weird woman who struck up a conversation with Sarah. A foot passenger from Saltspring, you know the type, a post-post-post hippie. A real space cadet. She was teaching Sarah a song, something folky about death.

"Scott was off on the other side of the cabin, reading a book, as you might expect.

"So she sees me watching her and Sarah, right? I guess I'm looking at her disapprovingly or something. But Sarah's getting off on it, learning this spooky little song.

"Anyway, she comes over, this woman, and starts talking to me as if we're old friends or something. Well, not quite. First thing she says—in this completely spaced-out voice—is 'Once I knocked on the door of a house in Hamilton, Ontario. I was looking for someone, but I had the wrong address. Anyway, this man answered the door. He was pointing a gun at me.' 'What happened?' I said. 'Nothing,' she said. 'I just turned and walked away. Nothing happened.'

"Then she says, 'I think I know your husband; he's that guy sitting over there, right?' And I said yes; she was pointing right at Scott. Of course she could have seen us at the terminal, or when we first came into the cabin, but I didn't think of that at the time. And then she says, 'I bet I can tell you his sign. He's a Capricorn, right?' Which he is, as you know. And then I started to get scared, Eric.

"I knew it was totally irrational, but I had this feeling that she'd somehow bewitched Sarah or something, and she knew who Scott was from another life or whatever, and she was going to take both of them away from me forever. It was terrifying. It really was.

"And then she asked if we could give her a ride from Tsawwassen into Vancouver, and I said 'No, we've got the car loaded up with stuff, there's hardly room for us.'

"And this woman just smiles sweetly and says, 'Oh yeah, I get the picture, see you around.' And she goes off out on the deck, and I never see her again."

"Did you ask Scott about her?"

"Yes, he said he'd seen us talking and wondered who she was. Some friend of mine, he'd thought. He said he'd never seen her before, either. It was really creepy. I can't explain it."

It's not like her to get worked up about something like this. Is this a sign of mental instability? (And my mother *will* ask about this sort of thing later. "Their situation," she'll say, must be a real... *strain* on Renee. Was there any indication...?" And her voice will trail off as she waits for me to supply precisely this sort of detail.)

I'm relieved when Scott and Sarah come back. Sarah wants to chat. What sort of house do I live in?

Renee is ready for this, perhaps has planned her intervention.

"Uncle Eric has a big house like the rich people in Oak Bay, except he lives back east, in Ontario, where the rich people are even richer."

Can this be good for a kid, I wonder, to be introduced to class warfare at her age?

I say, "Maybe one day you'll have a lot of money and have your own house in Oak Bay." It's possible, dammit. Look at me.

"Yeah, maybe," Sarah says, totally without conviction.

"There are more important things than money," Renee says.

Once I was going to be a poet. I wasn't bad at it, for a while. But then I realized I was only imitating the poets I admired, so what was the point. Scott thinks it's different with him and philosophy. Maybe it is, though the odds are against it. We can never talk about this directly.

I take them out to dinner, a restaurant suggested by Renee, the décor striving to embody some dim-witted Rotarian's idea of British Heritage, and the young female servers in peasanty-look-ing costumes clearly embarrassed about it—that sort of thing. The place is nearly empty. The kids are along, of course, making adult conversation very difficult, probably a blessing. For quite some time Scott says almost nothing, except to tell Geoffrey, who's five, not to do something. The kids chatter away, then, having sated themselves with a chocolate-based dessert concoc-tion, fall silent, too tired and bored to make a fuss.

Then Scott does start to talk. He talks about a book he's just finished reading, something about the aesthetics of modern architecture, nothing to do with his field. It soon becomes evi-dent that he's summarizing it, chapter by chapter. There's no opportunity for dialogue. Scott keeps going, right on through to the index.

Later we're back at their place, the kids in bed. We've been together forever. I've been in the same living room in Calgary, in Halifax, in Saskatoon. We have our repertoire of standing jokes, of innocuous things to make light of. Scott and I have embarrassing stories from remotest childhood to tell on each other, though the good ones have been recycled too often, as have Renee's multitudinous anecdotes of Scott's weirdness.

And then there's Scott's tragicomic academic career. His dissertation topic had to do with the use in philosophy of the concepts of clarity and vagueness. Once, at a community college job interview, bored by an obviously unprepared interrogator, he answered a question by saying only that his topic was vagueness. "Vagueness," said the interviewer, "I've never heard of him. Is he Swedish?" And so the three of us have, over the years, assembled the biography of Olaf Vagueness, the gloomy Scandinavian existentialist, whose personality overlaps significantly with Scott's. And whose career is, similarly, a saga of failure. Scott, oddly, enjoys this sort of thing—his sense of self is too strong for him to be concerned by teasing by the likes of Renee and me.

Yes, we've devised ways of getting along, of getting through. We're family.

"So," Renee is saying after a silence, "What are you going to tell her this time? Have we passed muster? Are we up to scratch? Will she ever give us money?" Scott flinches as she says this. "What do we have to do before she'll give us money?"

"I've never discussed that sort of thing with her. Honestly."

"Does she know that we have two children to feed and clothe? Does she know that Scott can't get employment because the system screws everybody who threatens its mediocrity? Is she aware of those facts?"

I know better than to use this moment to volunteer, once again, to provide assistance. Scott is glaring at me, as if daring me to do just that.

Renee announces that she's going to bed. She has to go to work in the morning, she reminds us.

Scott still hasn't said anything. Renee stumbles a bit as she passes the couch I'm sitting on, under the Bosch inferno.

"Good night, Mr. Businessman. Scott has told me you used to be a poet," she says as an exit line, one that she's probably been saving up since before I arrived.

Scott raises his eyebrows. Waits twenty seconds. "A bit too much to drink. She's not used to it."

"Let me tell you about poetry," I say. Yes, I'm that petty. "Here's a poem for you. Goneril Industries. Their real name, not ironic. The people who ran it didn't do irony. Big sugar people. Sugar and auto parts, actually. But mostly sugar. Just before Easter a little bird told me they were going to be taken over by even bigger sugar people."

I pause here to make sure he's paying attention.

"Survival of the sweetest," he says, pleased with himself.

"Very witty. In any case, what I'm talking about here is a hundred grand created out of thin air. In a week. Because I listened to the little bird. That's *my* poem. So. For the last time this trip. Do you need some money, or not?"

After the briefest of hesitations, he says, "No. No, I don't need it."

"I" not "we"—if that's not my brother, nothing is.

A little later he says he has to do some work on the computer. He gives me a blanket and a pillow for the couch.

For a long time I can't sleep. He's not making noise, but the room he's working in doesn't have a door, and too much light gets through to the living room. Worse than that, he's got the heat turned away up, maybe to show me that he can afford it. But I won't give him the satisfaction of having to listen to his little brother complain.

Let him tinker away on his keyboard, coolly efficient. Mr. Spock at the controls in the dead of night. Yes, he is the dedicated one. In a way I'm not, certainly. And I know Bosch's hell is poised above me. But what sin have I committed? I would be my brother's keeper if he'd let me. My conscience should be clear.

In the morning the kids wake. I'm vulnerable, an anomalous lump on the couch, and they attack with appropriate gusto. I respond with avuncular groaning and writhing. Renee is sourly polite, not wanting to spoil the kids' fun but letting me know there's no forgiveness. I guess I'm the enemy after all—a collaborator, the kind they hang from lampposts at the end of the war. By the time I've showered, Scott has joined the party, acknowledging my existence with a raised right eyebrow and an ambiguous shrug in the direction of the toaster. It's possible that he hasn't slept at all.

After prolonged goodbyes with Sarah and Geoffrey—it's understood that I'll be gone by the time they come home—mother and kids are off to school, leaving Scott and me with, yet again, nothing to say to each other.

Is there anything he'd like to do, I ask him. We've got my rented car, we could run errands or whatever. No, he says, there's nothing.

Then he disappears and comes back with a manuscript, a chapter, or part of one, from the book he's been working on.

"I'd value your opinion," he says, lying. "Do you mind? I'll make some more coffee."

It's about twenty pages. We both know I'll understand only a fraction of it. But at least we won't have to pretend to make conversation while I'm reading it, and he will have shown me again that he can do something that I can't.

When I've finished, I say what I'm supposed to say, something complimentary that both acknowledges my own ignorance and also has an ironic edge to it. Otherwise he'd know I was being patronizing.

Then he asks me a specific question, about how he attacked someone else's argument. It's a test. Have I read it carefully or have I been faking it?

"It struck me," I say, "that your position is very close to his, as far as I could understand it. I'm not sure why your disagreement with him seems so violent. That section on philosophical language about death. Aren't you splitting hairs?"

"My vision," he says, "is somewhat darker than his."

"You're a visionary now?" I shouldn't have said that. Something in his face makes me flash back to the moment yesterday when I wondered if he was capable of murder. His mouth seems to be about to break into a smile, and then it decides not to.

"Since you ask. Yes, I am."

And that's it. Of course he's not capable of murder. We'll have a last cup of coffee, to be consumed mostly in silence, and I'll be off. We'll do no physical harm to each other. We'll speak, when we need to, in civil tones.

Later, on the ferry, I'm sitting in a lounge area near the cafeteria where rows of chairs face each other. There's no one directly opposite me, but I half-expect there soon will be.

Sure enough, I'm still eating the sandwich when she shows up, the woman Renee talked about or her clone, the archetypal foot passenger from Saltspring, long dark hair, long dark dress decorated with odd white markings—runes, perhaps, or esoteric symbols. Her age? Maybe thirty, maybe fifty. As she sits down, I catch a glimpse of pale thigh, despite the dress, surely a deliberate gesture. She's thin, scary thin, emaciation festering in every pore. She looks at me directly and smiles. She has nothing to say, for the moment.

But soon she will start to speak. It's conceivable that she'll tell me that her name is Sky or Tree. Maybe she'll tell me that she's recently attended an alternative medicine conference in Oregon where she was turned on to iridology or reflexology or Rolfing. Possibly crystals will have been involved.

Maybe she'll try to sell me some drugs. Or maybe she'll simply ask if I'll give her a ride from Tsawwassen into Vancouver. And perhaps this will lead in turn to implied or explicit promise of casual meaningless sex. Or perhaps not.

But she has chosen me, in some sense.

And I think of what I would like to say to her, and will perhaps say, though in different words.

I know you, I would say. I know who you are. My brother would think that he knows you, but he doesn't. My sister-in-law is right to fear you. She doesn't know that it's too late, that my brother, who will never, technically, be unfaithful to her, has given himself to you irrevocably.

You who turn death into children's songs, you who have offered me paradise in many forms. I will not listen to you. I know lies when I hear them. I know who you are.

WHAT MY WIFE SAYS

Saturday, August 11, 1990

After the party my wife tells me that Eddie Laskowski has said that we should go out to their place sometime this summer. Eddie regrets the fact that his wife had to stay home tonight (they weren't able to get a babysitter), and thinks it would be nice if the four of us could spend some time together. When we go, I should bring my baseball glove along—Eddie knows I have a glove, I've boasted to him that I've had the same glove since I was fourteen—and Eddie and I will throw the ball around while my wife and Eddie's will sit on the deck and talk.

This proposal is insulting in a couple of ways, my wife explains. In the first place she doesn't know Eddie's wife at all, so why does Eddie assume they'll have such a lot to talk about? Secondly, what if *she*, my wife, wanted to throw the ball around with Eddie and me? Why would Eddie assume that she wouldn't find as much pleasure in this activity as a man? What sort of bizarre sexist stereotyping underlies Eddie's absurd suggestion? It's embarrassing, isn't it, to have to spell it out? Eddie Laskowski is, in my wife's opinion, an anachronism. She has no way of knowing what weird accident of historical happenstance has allowed his ilk to survive into the twenty-first century, but as far as she is concerned... etc., etc.

Of course in a way she's right, but I can't help feeling sorry for Eddie all the same. He means well, Eddie does, and he's been in trouble over this sort of thing before. He did his doctorate at a university in the southern US, and just after moving here he greeted two female members of our department as "ladies." I guess they still do that in parts of the southern US. One of the female colleagues took exception, at some length. Eddie confided to me later that this confused and hurt him; he was only trying to be courteous. The other incident occurred during a departmental seminar. Discussing some literary text or other, doing his best to navigate through one of the many minefields that "gender studies" have brought into being, he referred to the members of a certain subculture (if that is the correct term) as "deviants," although as soon as he said it, he must have sensed that he'd made a mistake. After a longish pause, he added the phrase "from the statistical norm," in a futile attempt to cover his ass. This is the sort of incident that makes good anecdotal compost: Eddie Laskowski is so backward that he actually *thinks*... blah blah blah.

Remembering this, I say to my wife: Poor Eddie. Well, at least it'll make a good story for your feminist friends.

Poor Eddie? Why poor Eddie? And what feminist friends? And what do I mean "good story"?

What I mean is that my wife will enjoy retailing this material about Eddie's invitation and the baseball glove—especially the baseball glove!—to like-minded women who will hoot, jeer, cluck, or guffaw at Eddie's innocent but apparently sinister idea that we should engage in bland, friendly social interaction. That's what I mean. I try to explain this as tactfully as possible.

By "feminist friends," I mean primarily Andrea and Emily, but there are others. (And here I rhyme off several additional names.) I am not using feminist as a term of derogation, I point out. Far from it.

My wife says never mind that shit, what exactly am I accusing her of? Using her commitment to feminism as an excuse to denigrate my friend Eddie? Really?

Well, is she *denying* that she might tell her friends this story about Eddie for its amusement value?

Yes, she is, in fact. She's not that sort of person.

What sort of person? Aren't we *all* that sort of person, to some degree? Don't we all derive pleasure from discussing the foibles and peccadilloes of others? Isn't it true, for example that she and Emily have this one friend, Jennifer, whose sole function as a friend is to say pretentious and condescending things so that she (my wife) and Emily can make fun of her (Jennifer) behind her (Jennifer's) back?

No, that's not true at all. Jennifer has many good qualities, which she and Emily are always quick to acknowledge. And she doesn't like the way we're drifting off the point.

What is the point?

The point, she says, is this. Has it ever occurred to me that I am a pig, a far grosser parody of humanity than Eddie Laskowski, benighted as he is, has ever dreamed of being? If not, perhaps I should have the honesty to confront this fact forthwith. She goes on to say a number of other things in this vein.

Sunday

Fortunately my wife does not hold grudges. By the time Andrea calls, early in the evening, I've been more or less forgiven. I make a point of not eavesdropping. But I do get a recap of their conversation later on.

Andrea wants to meet my wife after work tomorrow to tell her something really important, something so momentous she didn't want to discuss it over the phone. My wife has the impression that Andrea was afraid that Dick might come into the room while they were talking. It could be one of four things, my wife speculates: they can't make their mortgage payment; Andrea is pregnant; Andrea has discovered she's gay; Andrea has a male lover. Which is it, she wonders.

My own suggestions are: mortgage, three to one; pregnancy, four to one; gay, six to one; fooling around on Dick with another guy, four hundred to one.

Why is *that* such a long shot, my wife wants to know.

Well, Andrea is a wonderful person, but she doesn't seem to like men all that much. In general, I mean.

My wife's eyes narrow to slits. I can feel an abyss opening up in the middle of the living room.

And then, I add, there's the fact that a serious woman like Andrea, having entered into a long-term relationship with a man, would hardly be likely to jeopardize it by starting a frivolous affair. If she wanted to be with a man in the first place, I add, where would she find a better one than Dick? It just wouldn't make sense, would it? And as for not liking men in general, well, that's not a criticism of Andrea but simply an acknowledgement of her good taste and common sense. Who in her right mind *would* like men in general, I ask. Men: the gender that produced Genghis Khan, Hitler, Eddie Laskowski.

My wife waits for me to finish and then simply says, You're pathetic.

Monday

It's my turn to prepare dinner, pork chops, my wife's favourite. Today our schedule is thrown off by her rendezvous with Andrea. She calls from The Ship to say that she'll be longer than anticipated but I can go ahead and eat if I like. But I decide to wait.

When she comes in, she says that what Andrea has told her really is a secret, and there's no way she's going to reveal it to the likes of me. (The "likes" of me? I have likes?) Thank God there's an excellent chance that Andrea will come through it okay. But wild horses wouldn't drag a syllable out of her, so I might as well forget about it. Though *if* the secret ever becomes public knowledge, I'll be reminded of who knew about it long before anyone else in this household.

I ask her if Eddie Laskowski's name came up at all.

Eddie Laskowski, she says, is not worth a thought at this moment of crisis in Andrea's life. Where, she wants to know, are the pork chops?

Tuesday

Today's news. Jill has just accepted a teaching job in Northern Ontario, so there's going to be a party for her on Friday, at the place where Sandra is house-sitting, women only, so I might remember to bear that in mind in devising my weekend schedule of social engagements. Maybe, my wife suggests playfully, Eddie Laskowski and I could get together and organize some macho activity like a poker game.

I explain patiently that she is in danger of falling into grave error in interpreting Eddie Laskowski. Eddie regards poker as a waste of time, just as I do. He is, I point out, devoted to his family. He respects his wife's decision to stay home while the children are young, even though a family of four has a rough go of it on an assistant professor's salary.

My wife responds that my use of the phrase "respects his wife's decision" is problematic, to say the least. In all likelihood

Eddie has forced her to agree to abandon the prospect of a fulfilling career so that he can live out his archaic dream: to be the patriarch of a North American nuclear family from out of the fifties.

Wrong, I tell her. Eddie's a romantic. Has my wife not heard the story of how Eddie met his wife? How he and a buddy spent the summer after his second year of university backpacking around Europe, how he found his wife-to-be on a beach somewhere in Greece or Spain, fell deeply and powerfully in love with her—yes, "in love," one should not be ashamed to call something by its right name—and went with her back to her home country in Scandinavia (Sweden? Norway? I can never remember), where he learned the language (get that? learned the freaking impossible Scandinavian language) and finished his undergraduate degree over there, giving up—can my wife understand the poignancy of this sacrifice?—giving up the chance to play intercollegiate basketball in Canada. If that isn't altruistic romantic love to the nth degree, I'd like to know what is.

For once, she has nothing to say. At least, not about that.

Wednesday

After dinner my wife goes down to the basement and comes back up wielding a baseball glove I've never seen before. She says it's hers, been stashed down there since we moved in. It may be news to me, but she used to throw a baseball around a lot with Gary, of whom I have heard her speak many times.

All too many, I say quickly.

So, she wants to know, are we going over to the park for a game of catch or are we going to sit around all night like a couple of sedentary wimps? She just wants to know which it's going to be.

It wouldn't be pertinent to comment in detail on my wife's performance at the park. E for Effort might cover it. As we're walking home I ask her how I stack up against Gary as a catch-playing partner. She says his throws were easier to handle, if I follow her drift. I catch her chuckling to herself several times as we come down our street.

Later she says if that fascist Laskowski ever does invite us over, she'll be ready for him now. She won't be sitting in any damn rocking chair with his boring, docile cow of a wife, not when there's a ball game to be played.

Thursday

Emily lives in Toronto now, my wife reminds me, and she doesn't really know Andrea anyway, so it wouldn't be betraying any confidences to phone her (Emily) up and discuss her (Andrea's) situation, would it? My wife would really value Emily's input on this one. Especially if Andrea were to seek my wife's advice at some point in the probably very near future. It's something of a burden, having this kind of secret, burden as in knapsack with a lead weight in it strapped to your back. And who else is there, other than Emily? Me? Don't make her laugh.

Later in the evening I am informed that as far as the Andrea situation is concerned, Emily agrees with my wife one hundred per cent about what Andrea should do, but that's as much as I'm going to find out, so there's no point in resorting to my customary Gestapo interrogation tactics.

Also, Emily agrees with her about Eddie Laskowski, if I want to reopen that very tiresome can of worms.

Not really, I say. I've done my best to defend him. And I acknowledge that he has his weaknesses. For example, once when we were talking about women's tennis... Oh never mind. I myself am afflicted by no prejudices concerning the sexuality of professional female tennis players. While it would be an overstatement to say that some of my best friends are lesbians, it would certainly not shock or disgust me to learn that one of my *wife's* best friends...

If I'm fishing for info about Andrea, I'm barking up the wrong stream, my wife tells me. She realizes now that it was a mistake to confide in me in the first place.

Friday

My wife leaves for Jill's party around nine. Although Jill won't be moving to Northern Ontario for some weeks, everyone is bringing her going-away presents, some practical, some jokey. My wife regrets that Andrea thought of the condoms idea first.

As usual, the house seems very quiet after my wife has left. I do some reading, put a load of laundry on, watch the news. Then

I decide to go out for a short walk. My wife has given me the address of the house where the party is to be held—it's only a couple of blocks away—and more or less accidentally, I happen to pass by it.

The windows are all dark. It's silent. Not a sign of life.

What the hell's going on, I wonder. Are they having a séance? Have they all fallen asleep?

I walk up to the front door. Still no sound from inside.

What are the possibilities? Perhaps my wife has gone to incredible lengths to deceive me—but in that case, why give me an address so close to our own? Unless, of course, *she was hoping that I would discover the deception.* Or: the party *had been* here but (a) something horrible has happened to one or more of the women and they've all gone to the hospital; (b) they've gone off to conduct some weird bacchanalian ritual, something Andrea found a description of in a book, probably; (c) other.

I put my ear against the door just long enough to think how ridiculous I'd look to a passerby. In my heart I believe that nothing untoward has happened. A credible explanation will be forthcoming. If I go back home now, I can probably catch the last few innings of a ball game.

Which I do, but then still no sign of her. Determined to wait it out, I plunge back into my book.

Shortly after two, she waltzes in. She's had a fair bit to drink, it's clear, but nothing serious. She starts to tell me about the party, how much fun it was.

But where, I start to ask.

But the best part of the evening was the trip out to Three Pond Barrens for a moonlight swim. Olivia, who has a van, arrived later than the others, because she had to work late. When the question of swimming came up, she was still sober enough to drive. Of course they didn't have suits, but this added to the sense of adventure. So they piled into the van with their cases of beer and bottles of wine, and headed on out.

It was chilly at first, my wife says, but once you got in, it was really warm. It was interesting, too, to see everyone nude, people you always think of as wearing clothes. Do I know what she means? It's as though they're suddenly different people, or the world is different, or something. It was really warm once you got in, she tells me again.

As I hug her I can feel some sort of residual chill coming from her skin, and I keep holding her as she goes on to tell me about the nine nude women laughing and splashing in the moonlit water.

BRICK

Vince and Isabel, Canadian snowbirds, for some years now have spent their winters in Zero Beach, Florida. One year Vince, an accomplished do-it-yourselfer, decided to expand the perimeter of their backyard patio by two feet or so, in order to be better able to catch the sun early in the day. He finished the job not long after Christmas. It wasn't a major project, but Vince was a meticulous worker, always striving for perfection, and, as he surveyed his handiwork, he felt a powerful sense of achievement. The bricks were aligned flawlessly. There was an intrinsic beauty to their pattern, a testament to human ability to impose aesthetically pleasing order on the randomness of the natural world. Mission accomplished!

Next morning Vince, relaxing on the patio with an after-breakfast coffee, noticed something unusual. One of the recently positioned bricks near the edge of the patio was slightly out of place. It was tilted upward, its full length balanced against one of its neighbours, like a miniature Leaning Tower of Pisa. A minor mystery, though even to call it that would be to magnify its importance in the eyes of most people. But not Vince, an inveterate seeker of truth, though he would be too modest to claim such a lofty title for himself. How had this happened? He wanted an answer.

First he called Isabel out to take a look. While not as keen to solve the puzzle as he was, she recognized that this was the sort of thing that could preoccupy Vince for hours, if not days. Maybe they should get this settled as quickly as they could. And so they discussed the obvious possibilities. Maybe it was a mole? But there were no other signs of mole-related activity, moles were not known to frequent their backyard, and it was hard to picture a mole inadvertently shifting a brick to its current unnatural position.

It seemed more likely that human agency would be involved. But in what form and to what end? Neighbourhood kids? Unlikely—there weren't any kids living in the immediate vicinity, and why would kids, presumably bent on making mischief, dislodge a single brick from Vince and Isabel's patio and leave it at that? Further, there were no other signs that anything was amiss in the backyard, nothing broken, damaged, or stolen, no footprints, cigarette butts, or beer cans. Not a blade of grass had been disturbed, as far as Vince and Isabel could tell.

Okay, perhaps it was a kid or kids simply cutting through the backyard? One of them steps on the brick, which had not been fitted in as snugly as Vince had thought, and up it pops? No, this was so clearly not the case that it didn't come up for discussion. There were fences separating Vince and Isabel's property from those of the people on either side. And at the back there was a higher chain-link fence blocking the way to an assisted living facility. So whoever or whatever moved the brick, it would not have been in the course of passing through.

So. The backyard, the patio, the brick, had been someone's destination. The creepiest of hypotheses would identify the culprit as a burglar or home invader who checked things out and then decided to abort the mission. But this one wasn't fully convincing either. What potential intruder in the middle of the night takes the time to reach down, pick up a random brick from a patio and place it carefully so that the next day the house-holder will notice it sticking up?

Maybe, Isabel suggested, he sort of tripped on the edge of the brick, forcing it upward, and then, struggling to retain his balance, twisted it to one side but not with sufficient force to knock it right over. Hence its current otherwise-inexplicable posture. Neither she nor Vince believed this theory, but neither could think of anything more to say. An unimportant, probably unsolvable mystery, they tacitly agreed. Time to move on.

Vince got up and put the brick back where it should have been, tight against the two adjoining it. Order restored. Later that day he checked with the neighbours. Nothing untoward had taken place in their backyards. Charlie Hoskins was amused at the notion that Vince would be concerned about it. "Could've been a million things did it," Charlie opined. "Wouldn't give it a second thought, myself." Charlie was eighty-five or so, and hard of hearing. Vince felt disappointed that he had been unable to explain clearly the distinction between a brick that had somehow become slightly dislodged and one that had undoubtedly been deliberately moved to a near-upright position. The widow on the other side, a Mrs. Codrington, expressed alarm at the thought of someone "out there in the dark," as she put it. Perhaps the police should be called? As she said this, Vince realized how absurd his concern would seem to a generic Zero Beach patrol officer, with his dark glasses, prominently displayed firearm, and impatient stance. Vince would be on the receiving end of pity or contempt, or (most likely) both. No thanks, he thought. And didn't think much more about it after that.

But three or four days later, it happened again. Same brick, same precarious positioning—leaning up against the brick beside it. As before, nothing else in the yard had been disturbed. Vince felt a twinge of anger, which he immediately suppressed. Someone was messing with him, and he didn't like it, but he knew that the best response was to remain calm and rational. Was some sort of message being sent? But if so, what could it be? Someone, in the dead of night, had not once but twice crept into his backyard, apparently simply to demonstrate that it could be done. But there was no news there, surely. It was the sort of gesture that could only inspire a response of "So what?" What we have here, Vince thought, is a failure to communicate. And smiled at the thought of Paul Newman as Cool Hand Luke tiptoeing into the yard to disturb a single brick. When he told her about it, Isabel, fortunately, was unfazed. It's probably a joke, was her take. Sooner or later the prankster will reveal himself. In the meantime let's just ignore it.

But of course Vince couldn't let it go. For the next few evenings he kept vigil from inside the house, eyes glued to the backyard from sundown until at least midnight, and then getting up at six to see if he couldn't catch the guy (because it wouldn't be a woman, would it?) red-handed or brick-handed, perhaps a harmless eccentric, himself an early riser, Vince speculated, with a strange sense of humour. Perhaps the point of moving the brick was that there was no point, a bit of performance art proclaiming the arbitrariness of the human condition. Or something like that.

For four or five nights nothing happened. Then there came a night when Vince had a vivid dream (of which more later) and maybe because of that (who knows) he slept in, until nine. Had Isabel checked the patio? No, of course not. She'd thought they were done with that silliness. Vince was out the back door in no time.

And, as you may have guessed, there it was. But with a difference. The brick wasn't leaning against the next one this time but was lying across the space it had occupied, its ends resting on top of the bricks adjacent to it, a bridge from nowhere to nowhere.

We now require a broader context. My third-person voice has been treating this material as though the world ended at Vince and Isabel's property line, and I've been deliberately vague about certain details. For example, I've said that the action of my story begins shortly after Christmas but didn't say which one, creating, I've imagined, a parable-like sense of timelessness. But now we need to immerse ourselves in facts.

A little before 12:55 p.m. Eastern Standard Time on a January day not long ago, a young man whose name does not need to be recorded here, having arrived at Fort Lauderdale-Hollywood International Airport on a Delta flight from Minneapolis, retrieved his one piece of luggage from the baggage claim area in Terminal 2 and carried it into a nearby washroom. Shortly thereafter he emerged with a Walther PPS semi-automatic pistol tucked into his waistband. I believe there is video footage, though I haven't seen it myself, of him pulling out his pistol and beginning to fire. He was apparently aiming at people's heads, the victims, as far as anyone could tell, chosen at random. Eyewitness accounts are as depressing as they are predictable. The young man said nothing, showed no emotion, appeared to be in a trancelike state. It was not clear how it was possible, said one survivor, that the people all around him had been hit but he had been spared. Pure luck, he guessed. The shooting lasted sixty to eighty seconds, at which point the young man ran out of ammunition. He then lay down on the floor near a baggage carousel and waited to be apprehended. He had killed five people and wounded six; in addition, some three dozen others had been injured in the chaos as they scrambled to escape.

Vince and Isabel saw the coverage on the evening news. Like many others, one suspects, they didn't say much to each other about it. It was the time of Orlando, Nice, Brussels, Paris, San

Bernardino. If the names of these cities, in conjunction with each other, mean nothing to you, reader, count yourself fortunate. You've outlived the need to remember (or learn about) a particular season of evil that others have no choice but to remember. What was there for Vince and Isabel to say? One feels a quick shiver of empathy for the victims and their families, notes with relief that the gunman has already been deemed mentally disturbed as opposed to being a real terrorist, and one moves on.

In the Zero Beach newspaper the next day, there was an interview with a local woman who had been present during the carnage. Mrs. Doris Throckmorton, forty-nine, self-identified as a born-again Christian, a member of a Baptist congregation. She'd been on the same flight as the gunman, she said. She'd just collected her luggage from the carousel when the shooting began. She reported being unable to move as the man walked calmly in her direction, firing at and hitting people near where she was standing. She'd been sure that she'd be next. Then, she said, she'd remembered to pray, a short prayer from the depths of her heart. She had so much to live for! (A brief catalogue of her "loved ones" followed.) She gave the Lord a quick reminder that His mercy is infinite. But now the gunman was getting closer, was taking aim directly at her. She thought that the whispered words "Praise you, Jesus" would be the last that she would ever utter. And then, inexplicably, the pistol aimed at her head swerved to her left. "The poor man next to me went down like a sack of potatoes," Mrs. Throckmorton told the reporter. "I don't think he made it." Her husband, Clyde, had been standing near her on her

104 • LARRY MATHEWS

right. "I guess my prayer worked for him, too," she added. "It all just goes to show how important it is to get right with the Lord."

Her bland, innocent, unremarkable face in the newspaper photo seemed to Vince to radiate a certain complacent self-satisfaction. Though perhaps, he thought, that was being uncharitable.

I've already mentioned that Vince doesn't like to be messed with. While Mrs. Throckmorton's account of her experience was of course not directed specifically to him, Vince did take it personally, representing, as he felt he did, Christian believers who, while passionate about their faith, also happened to be intelligent, well-informed, rational, reasonably sophisticated. The ignorance, the boneheaded self-centred ignorance was what got to him. Sure, she was probably still in a state of shock when she did the interview, allowances could be made, but still, consider the woman's basic mindset. The character of the Creator of the universe is such that he can be verbally manipulated by a person so benighted that she can cheerfully accept her own miraculous deliverance at the cost of the life of the innocent man next to her, accept it without batting a proverbial eye, interpreting the event as something that "goes to show" the truth of some threadbare theological banality that she had been taught to parrot.

Isabel listened patiently. She knew what was coming next. Vince had a long history of writing letters to editors, indignant, impassioned but coherent arguments on various topics which sometimes, to her surprise, actually got published, though most often in a truncated form. She would keep her distance while Vince tapped relentlessly away at his laptop.

He decided, early on, not to reveal himself as a Catholic. To present the issue as Catholic (superior) vs. Protestant (inferior) would be reductive, would simply encourage readers to reaffirm their allegiance to whichever side of the divide they belonged on. And would turn off all the others. In fact concealing his Catholicism would allow him a certain freedom. He could argue on the basis of common sense, for example. He could risk being heretical if it served his purpose. He began to enjoy himself.

I won't reproduce the text of Vince's letter. Instead I'll simply insist that sometimes truth is easier to discern in the form of summary or of highlight than in the pedestrian slog of A-to-Z comprehensiveness. But I've left a trail of breadcrumbs if you want to go that route. There's a local newspaper in the community that I've coyly misnamed "Zero Beach," and they have a website that you can google and check to see whether my account is accurate. But that would take more time than you probably have, and I hope that by now I've earned your trust.

Vince presented himself as someone who, though not an adherent of any particular religious organization, was a spiritual person, someone who believed that the cosmos was permeated by a divine presence that would forever elude human understanding. Further, he saw nothing wrong with Mrs. Throckmorton's decision, in her moment of fear, to launch a prayer into the void. But let's get real, Vince urged. Consider the five dead victims of the shooting. Were any of them praying (a real possibility, was it not?), and if so, what kind of God decides that Mrs. Throckmorton's prayer should be answered and theirs not? And suppose the victims didn't pray, and that was the deal-breaker, what kind of God puts the thought of praying into Mrs. Throckmorton's head but not theirs? And what kind of God makes that the deal-breaker in the first place? No, Vince continued, the notion that there is something out there, some *person* listening to prayers is bizarre enough. But the idea that such a person would have the power and the desire to intervene in the realm of cause and effect and change the outcome of a sequence of events that would otherwise be determined by human free will, well that, as far as he was concerned, was the real deal-breaker, the breaker of the deal we've made collectively with reason and common sense.

Vince was particularly pleased that he hadn't stooped to attack Mrs. Throckmorton's character. It would be for the readers of his letter to make the appropriate application. Fair-minded, objective people would be impressed, he thought, as he emailed the letter to the newspaper. It may or may not have been the next morning when Vince noticed the out-of-place brick for the first time. It didn't then occur to him to relate the two events.

A few days later the letter was published, having been somewhat shortened by an insensitive butcher of an editor. The following morning, Vince is pretty sure about this, was when he noticed that the brick had been moved for a second time. In the days that followed, there were no letters to the editor engaging with Vince's ideas, either supporting his position or attacking it. This happened a lot with Vince's letters to editors. After a day or so, he actually forgot about it.

And then, as mentioned above, there was the night of the dream. And I apologize in advance for it. We're obviously deep in Flannery O'Connor territory here, but as far as I can recall, she doesn't allow the climaxes of her stories to be in the form of dreams. She's too classy for that. Visions, yes, moments of profound revelation for her characters, yes, but not the paint-by-numbers cop-out of the dream. So my allegiance to truth compels me to go against the grain and make use of that rusted-out and badly dented literary cliché. (Notice how I avoided saying "hoariest"? I'm quite proud of that.)

It's a dream of no subtlety, no nuance, no complexity. Fortunately it can be summarized in a couple of sentences. Vince dreamed that he owned a huge ranch in Texas. He was sitting on his front porch, admiring the stone wall that he himself had built, a wall that he knew encompassed his entire property, though he could of course see only a portion of it from his vantage point. See what I mean about absence of subtlety? It gets worse. He was looking at the road leading to his front gate, feeling satisfied about the job he had done, when he noticed that a large stone had been removed from the wall near the gate and was now on the ground a few feet away. (It's not clear why whatever it was in the depths of Vince's psyche that was constructing the dream didn't go all the way and make it a *brick* wall.) In any case, this situation perplexed Vince, since he could recall having worked hard to ensure that every stone was securely berthed in its proper place. It's also not clear why Vince, owner of a vast cattle ranch, hadn't hired stonemasons to build his wall. And why Texas, where he'd never been? Dreams, who can figure 'em?

But the dream is not really the climax of this story.

Because Vince woke to find that the brick, the real-life brick from his patio, had been moved that third time.

But the thing is, a few mornings later, the brick had been moved again. Vince had not himself moved the brick from its "bridge" position, spanning the now-empty space where it should have been inserted. Something amused him about the idea of the bridge, like a minuscule Stonehenge, serving no practical purpose but declaring itself to be symbolic of... something. Of what, Vince wasn't sure, but the thought of it gave him a minor *frisson* of aesthetic pleasure.

But now that arrangement had been disrupted. The brick was now standing in the original Leaning Tower of Pisa configuration, as if something were saying, "Back to square one."

Vince decided that, if he were ever to make sense of what was happening to him, he would need to find a satisfying religious solution, a Catholic solution. He was old enough to remember the Catholicism of the fifties, when the Mass was in Latin, you couldn't eat meat on Fridays, nobody knew that belief in Limbo was optional, and the Rosary had only three kinds of Mystery (joyful, sorrowful, and glorious, if he remembered correctly). But now somehow there were four, or so he'd read somewhere.

Sometimes Vince looks back to that era with a certain nostalgia. Things related to the Church were clear and simple, as he now remembers it. Is there a Catholic of that era who didn't have an uncle who was a priest? (I use the past tense because they've nearly all died off by now.) Vince had one too, now long gone, who believed he could predict the length of time that people close to him would have to spend in Purgatory. In Vince's mother's case, the verdict was thirty-five years, which might be lessened somewhat if people prayed for her. He never found out how his uncle had made this calculation.

Vince wondered what his uncle would have to say about his own current situation, smiling at the ludicrous arrogance with which the black-and-whiteness of the issue of the brick would be spelled out for him. It was entirely possible that some demonic force would be declared to be involved. After all, whence came the inspiration for Vince's letter to the editor? How was that going to help anyone spiritually? And was Purgatory even a thing anymore? No one's mentioned it for years, decades. Yes, his uncle would say, it certainly is still "a thing." Forget the possibility that it's gone the way of meatless Fridays. But think, Vince, he could hear his uncle saying in his head, Think! How can the enigma of the peripatetic brick be moved beyond?

Because there it was, still pointing stubbornly skyward. Of course Vince could knock it over any time he felt like it. But what would that prove?

Vince sat on his comfortable chair on the patio, drinking his coffee, listening to his uncle's imagined voice. His uncle must know more now, he thought, than he did when he was alive. Would it be superstitious or worse to just shut up and listen? No, he decided. It wouldn't.

The problem you're having, Vince, is that this story can't have a real climax, at least not something that can be rendered as having *happened*, definitively, once and for all, in the neat patterns of black-and-whiteness I loved so much when I was alive. In the post-O'Connor world of post-epiphany, which happens to be the one you're living in, you can't honestly bring things to an ordered conclusion. The brick will keep moving. That's the point.

And doesn't everyone have such a brick?

Your Texas stone wall has imprisoned you. Putting the dislodged stone back in place won't make you safer. There's something that can make a gun pointed at Mrs. Throckmorton's head move aside. Or it can make a patio brick stand on end. You can stay up as late as you like, but that something can outwait you. It exists. Better make your peace with it.

FLOWER HEAVEN

Okay Crystal, this is what I would tell you in keeping with my policy of absolute honesty in my personal life, a policy I had intended to put into practice on arriving in this city almost a year ago but have not yet quite been able to.

I'd start with this warm summer evening we're currently in the midst of (but there's always that sense, isn't there, of the vast cold above us, waiting to descend like a clenched fist), and I'd start by saying this.

"I began to hate Crystal's mother when I heard her outside my window one summer evening."

That's how I'd start. Then I'd just keep going. I'd use third person for objectivity, for distance. I wouldn't stop until I'd had my full say. I'd trust you, Crystal, to be paying attention.

• • •

She was talking. To her daughter, her grown daughter, Crystal, who lives upstairs.

I began to hate her because I realized that she was the source of all of her daughter's problems, or one of the main sources anyway, especially of the problems Crystal herself was only vaguely aware of.

Did I mention that I live in the basement? I don't have to live in a basement. I choose to live in this basement because of its proximity to my workplace. There are many apartment buildings farther away from my workplace that I could afford to live in, buildings offering ordinary above-ground accommodation.

Okay. So I live in Crystal's basement. Only it isn't really Crystal's. Her mother owns the house. I need to begin with that fact.

At the moment I began to hate her, she was speaking to Crystal, just outside one of my windows. She was discussing the flowerbed. Here is what she said to cause my loathing of her to rise to the level of consciousness. She said, "This poor flower has died and gone to flower heaven."

Innocuous enough, you're thinking. But it was the tone, not just the content. The tone was not sugary, sentimental. This was not the utterance of a naive woman, nor that of a dim-witted woman believing herself to be funny in some straightforwardly idiotic way. No, there was a gratuitous cynicism in the way she made this comment, gratuitous because the subject was after all no more abstruse than the frigging flowerbed. Nor was her irony directed merely at the conventional idea of heaven, a point one could have endorsed. No, it was clear from the way she enunciated this sentence that her aim was to attack and ridicule the very notion of spirituality itself. It simultaneously expressed anger at the condition of the universe as she understood it and functioned as a kind of victory cry celebrating her own hardness of heart at being able to accept this fact and continue to live her ultimately meaningless life.

"This poor flower has died and gone to flower heaven."

The world as I know it is shit, she might as well have said.

I felt intense anger on Crystal's behalf.

Women such as Crystal's mother are not uncommon. She had attached herself to a powerful man and devoted her life to manipulating him and their offspring. In Crystal's mother's case, the man was a successful local car dealer who had the vision to move the dealership to the suburbs at exactly the right time. Such women have no sense of how pathetically myopic their view of the world is.

And yet, and yet. Some force in the psyches of such women, some still small voice, to use the biblical cliché, keeps raising the question of meaning, of authenticity. Something keeps drawing their attention to the fact that their lives are empty—and if *their* lives are empty, so must everyone else's be, for the notion of quest, of self-discovery, of reorienting their lives, is utterly foreign to them. And so the voice must be answered, rebuked, rejected: what do you say, voice, to the fact of the death of this flower, of my own always-impending death; what do the spurious consolations of conventional religiosity, the harps and fluffy white clouds, mean now? Nothing.

Flower heaven. The absurd coquettishness of it. The self-congratulatory element. I've played the game, she was saying to the voice. I've seen through it all. Don't tell me that there is more to me, or to life. Just shut up.

My challenge is: to make Crystal understand all this.

Crystal is, at twenty-seven or so, studying criminology in the hopes of one day becoming a lawyer. (She has failed the LSATs once and will keep trying until she makes it through.) Although she dates frequently, she is unattached. She has travelled abroad. Her employment history includes stints as a secretary (the dealership) and as a cocktail waitress—jobs taken, she has told me, so that she could see how "the other half lives." My assessment is that her life is salvageable. But of course one can't simply knock on her door and deliver one's analysis of her situation.

Indeed, real conversation between us is rare. Even casual exchanges occur only about once a week. Our respective spaces don't overlap, except for the area near the back door, the basement stairs, and the laundry room. Oddly, our most significant point of contact stems from the fact that her bedroom is directly above where I have my TV, so when her TV is on at the same time as mine is, and on the same channel, our auditory domains flow suggestively into each other. Occasionally there's some action in the bed up there, too, but I try to ignore that. That way madness lies.

But what way does madness not lie? Sometimes I glance over my shoulder at the past, that tangled frozen thicket from which I have for the moment escaped, sanity barely intact. The future looms, a dark cave in a bleak hillside.

Then there's my job, which involves dealing with young people. How they sicken me, the young, with their ridiculous overestimation of their potential, their baseless optimism about their future lives, their inarticulate but firmly held belief that the world has been designed expressly for them. I do nothing to disabuse them of these notions. Life will kick them in the teeth soon enough.

Shortly after I moved in, Crystal informed me of her interest in criminology, and forced a copy of *The Executioner's Song* upon me. If I liked that one, she said, she had a good book about Ted Bundy that I might like too.

I thought that this was somewhat strange, given the context of a single man moving into the basement apartment in the house of a single woman. It seemed somehow inauspicious. "Drawn together by fate and their mutual interest in serial killers…"? But then why should I have thought of our association as a potential love story? Me, of all people.

Crystal had done some work at the local pen, she said, as part of a class project. Maximum security. She knew a lot of murderers. They're ordinary guys who made a mistake, she said. It could happen to anyone. You, for example. If you commit a murder, don't talk to anybody until your lawyer comes. And don't feel bad about it. It's happened to a lot of decent guys.

It was hard to know how to take all this. Did she see all men as potential murderers, or was it me in particular? Or perhaps all of her basement tenants? And what had happened to the last guy who'd lived there, a man named Eric, to whom Crystal had referred once or twice in passing? And why wouldn't a semi-educated woman be capable of making some distinction between *The Executioner's Song* and "a good book about Ted Bundy"? None of these were questions that I felt free to ask her directly, sensing that she might regard any of them as in some way inappropriate.

As I contemplate the implications of Crystal's mother's remark about the flower, it occurs to me that in the approximately ten months I have lived here, Crystal and I have had only two real conversations.

One happened in the fall when we *were* watching the same movie on TV, *The Maltese Falcon*, and we both experienced the odd stereo effect with its all too symbolic component, the sound uniting our separate realms. Eventually she came down, knocked on my door, and invited me up.

To her bedroom. Turned out there was no chair handy to the TV, so I had to sit on a corner of her bed. Modestly dressing-gowned, she propped herself against the headboard, having given me a beer.

I was nervous, I admit. But she definitely wasn't coming on to me, for which I was grateful. Last thing I needed at that point in my life.

You seem nervous, she said.

Nervous? Me? Why do you say that?

She began to enumerate the obvious physical symptoms of nervousness that I was presenting. I became increasingly embarrassed. Then she seemed to lose interest in that subject.

Funny we should both be watching this, she said. You know, you remind me a bit of Peter Lorre.

Oh, that was promising. I thought briefly of trying to say something witty, perhaps by riffing on the phrase "a bit of Peter Lorre," but decided to hold my tongue. Banter does not come easily to me, and I doubted my ability to keep going beyond an initial exchange. It occurred to me that she was perhaps setting out to be deliberately provocative. Perhaps I was to be raw material for some academic project. Perhaps we were being taped.

I've never noticed any such resemblance myself, I informed her carefully. Nor has anyone else ever commented on it.

You've been dumped, haven't you, she said, out of nowhere. It wasn't even a question.

She was, in a sense, right, though not technically.

Why do you say that?

It's obvious. All alone all the time. You never have visitors. Never go out in the evenings. You go to work, you come home, you've got the TV or radio on all the time, your phone never rings. Plus you talk to yourself. I can hear you mumbling. And also you've got dumped written all over your sad-ass face.

I felt both dismayed and liberated. All my previous dealings with women had depended upon my constructing a certain persona, one whose makeup did not coincide with the constellation of qualities Crystal had just outlined. I realized that the whole issue of persona-construction was now moot, as far as she was concerned. By the same token, I was now absolved of any need to attempt such construction.

Still, I felt an atavistic need to defend myself.

I don't think I mumble, I said. Sometimes I find it useful to say things out loud, about issues that come up at work. I like to plan what I should say ahead of time. I like to make myself clear.

But the point is, you've been dumped.

Technically that's not the case.

What do you mean, technically?

Never mind.

Tell me about her.

No, I don't think so.

Tell me about your life, then.

No. Maybe another time.

It's true that I was being less than completely open with Crystal here, and I myself was somewhat disappointed with my performance. I was able to console myself with the thought that I had at least avoided telling her any lies.

Okay, she said. I'll tell you about me, then.

Which she did, for approximately half an hour. Her parents, relationships, career plans, the usual suspects. She was, I quickly came to realize, a bland woman, a woman of no intrinsic interest whatsoever. But she was also, of course, a fellow human being, and I felt sad as I thought about her future: what an easy life it was going to be for her, how everything she encountered would slowly be engulfed by her blandness, like some gooey off-white substance generated by aliens in a low-budget sci-fi flick from the fifties. How she would miss everything important about being alive.

So that's me, she said finally. I'd said almost nothing during her spiel. What do you think?

Sounds like a good life. Sounds like you're focused, you're motivated, you've got your shit together, you're going places.

Somehow candour had eluded me. Not that any of these statements were lies, exactly. In fact they all expressed a certain kind of truth, though not the important kind. But I said nothing about my sadness, and that omission was, I acknowledge, tantamount to a lie.

But you, she said. Before you go. 'Fess up—she dumped you, didn't she? Let me be frank here, an unprepossessing man like yourself doesn't get many chances, am I right? The odds of you dumping her are pretty slim, unless she's a real dog herself.

I said nothing. I thought "unprepossessing" was below the belt. Though I was pleasantly surprised that she knew the word. Even so, I was slightly hurt.

Unprepossessing? I said.

Hey, I'm just rattling your cage. Lighten up.

My cage. Food for thought there, I was thinking.

I was actually encouraged by this. I thought that Crystal was unexpectedly demonstrating the potential to transcend her blandness. But then I realized that the idea of rattling one's cage is a cliché in colloquial discourse; it was unlikely that she had, after careful reflection, decided that my situation was, metaphorically, that of an incarcerated beast. She would have made a similar comment to anyone she happened to be teasing.

The word "unprepossessing" gave me pause too. A Rorschach blot of a word, that one. Pre-possession: possession before. So un-pre-possession would imply no previous ownership, a fresh start, something I'd hoped to find in moving to this city. I doubted that Crystal had the imagination to see the subtlety. I suspected, too, that she would not listen attentively to any explanation I might offer.

But it is also true that I am an unprepossessing man, in the conventional sense. I acknowledge that.

• • •

That winter was the coldest I have ever experienced, though people told me that it was regarded by long-time denizens of the place as "tolerable" or even "half-decent." It was as though, having no knowledge of other cities, they had come to accept as normal what most of the planet's population would regard as an unprecedented lapse of competence on nature's part. I voiced this view, perhaps too frequently and insistently, at my workplace. I sensed that I was failing to gain acceptance from my co-workers.

Why does anyone live here? I would ask. What if everyone just moved somewhere else, where it's warmer?

I received no coherent answers to these questions.

I would march to work in pitch darkness, a fifteen-minute eternity of salt and carbon monoxide. I refused to wear a hat; it would have seemed too much like giving in to the world's brutal mindlessness. I recognized that living here was best regarded as some sort of test, which I was determined to pass. As a result I was plagued for much of the winter by a head cold, for which I took no medication.

At work, the young people with whom I was paid to interact grew more sullen and depressed with each passing week. When the morning blackness finally lifted, the sun shone too brightly, cruelly revealing the blotches and pits on their pallid faces, faces which nevertheless radiated a stubborn belief in their right to get more from life than they were ever likely to deserve.

January, February. Crystal developed an addiction to the music of Kate Bush. As though it weren't cold enough outside, I would have no choice but to hear, night after night, Kate Bush's voice cascading down into my space, a torrent of ice water, freezing Niagaras of it, indecipherable lyrics blending into each other in some Esperanto of female pain and longing.

I sensed that Crystal must be in some state of desperation, having glimpsed, over the wall of blandness that surrounded her, something new and dark, something that Kate Bush's screech could not keep at bay much longer.

Perhaps I could be of assistance, I thought, unprepossessing though I was. It occurred to me that I had seen even less of Crystal than usual these last few weeks. Perhaps I should make some gesture.

I made a special trip upstairs to return *The Executioner's Song*, to take her up on her longstanding offer regarding the "good book on Ted Bundy." Or maybe she'd have something else she thought might interest me, a recent bio of Jeffrey Dahmer, for example.

Her face was a *tabula rasa*. Nothing important has ever happened to me, it said. Nor could I discern any trace of inner turmoil as we spoke. Wasn't Gary Gilmore creepy, she wanted to know. Certainly gave her the creeps. But I should know that it made her feel safe to know that I was living just downstairs.

As casually as possible I mentioned Kate Bush.

Isn't she great? I always listen to her music in the dead of winter. It's so energetic, so strong, it gives *me* strength. It's funny. Eric noticed the same thing last winter.

Whatever happened to Eric, by the way?

Eric. Oh, he, um, he moved on. Butter wouldn't melt.

Perhaps—cartoon lightbulb in my head turned on—Eric had committed a murder. Eric was the prototypical ordinary guy who made a mistake, who didn't have the sense to shut up until his lawyer came, who had been visited in maximum security.

Dead of winter, indeed.

I noted that we were still standing at Crystal's kitchen door and that she'd made no move to invite me in. Also that neither of us had said anything while I was mulling over the Eric-as-murderer scenario. But I couldn't bring myself to ask the question. Another inexplicable failure of nerve on my part.

So I'll dig out that Ted Bundy book and give it to you tomorrow.

But the book never appeared.

• • •

In March an odd thing happened at work, having to do with my supervisor, a man only slightly older than me, a churchgoing fuss-budget family man whose small talk consisted almost entirely of brief expositions of the convoluted politics of church committees. Often these anecdotes would centre on the organist, a man whose first name was Alabaster.

"I was afraid Alabaster would be upset," my supervisor would say, "so I took it to the committee and they said, 'We've done all we can for Alabaster on this one, so if he's still unhappy, it's up to you to bring him around.' So I called Alabaster, feeling like a chump, and he said he wasn't happy but he could live with it, and I said, 'Alabaster, that's very understanding of you, very charitable,' and Alabaster said—and this is the umpteenth time I've heard him say it—'I just want to be a team player. Just tell the committee that Alabaster wants to be a team player here.'" And so forth.

What little acceptance I received from my co-workers came from my ability to imitate this man, his earnestness, this obsessive interest in conserving office supplies, his use of outdated colloquialisms.

On the Tuesday of the first week of March, he came to work with his hair dyed pink and announced to everyone that he and Alabaster were leaving that day for faraway Toronto, where they would begin a new life, together.

The rest of us sat there silently, most of my co-workers (losers they, almost to a person) no doubt thinking that he had finally "cracked" or "snapped," views that they would express loudly and repeatedly for the rest of the week. But for me it was a triumphant demonstration of how one's life could be changed in an instant.

How insensitive I had been. And how unthinkable for me to make a parallel gesture of my own (what would it be, anyway?)—and how blindly naive on my part to have thought that he simply liked the sound of the word "Alabaster" rather than the human reality it evoked for him.

Later that week a co-worker gave me a letter he'd found sticking out of a snowbank several blocks from where I lived. It had been addressed to me, with the street and number identified accurately but with the wrong postal code. The letter itself was of no importance (except symbolically—the apparent gratuitousness of the delivery, the timing), but the little drama that its snowbank presence implied enraged me. The laziness and cynicism of the postman (or woman), the deeper corruption of civic order that made permissible his or her decision to discard casually a document that for all he or she knew might contain verbal marvels, a *cri de cœur* perhaps, that would astonish and transform the recipient.

I briefly considered writing (irony, irony) *letters* to the postal authorities, to elected representatives, to the media—but quickly abandoned the idea, knowing the stupid intransigence which would manifest itself in response.

Within two weeks of the pink-haired supervisor's departure, it was as if he had never been there. When it was necessary to refer to him, he was "the guy who used to be here" or "the fella who left."

The city's media became fixated on the fortunes of its professional hockey team. It was as though someone in authority had decided that the rest of us, the general public, stolid, immobile, were to be granted this one vicarious dose of synthetic energy and imagination to sustain us until spring.

On Good Friday, feeling low-intensity self-hatred (how had I allowed things to come to this?), I watched the home squad defeat the worst team in their division, the proverbial cellar-dwellers, to clinch a playoff spot. A six-two win, a hat trick for the star right-winger. Whoopee. When I turned the TV off, I heard Crystal above me, in the throes of orgasm—or possibly faking it (who knew?).

On reflection, this account is not quite true. Life rarely offers such a pat concatenation of events, even events as trivial as these. It was, I think, the next night, or even Easter Sunday itself before I heard Crystal groaning in jubilant heat.

•••

In late April, after her exams were over, Crystal and a girlfriend flew south for ten days in the sun. I was charged with feeding the cats (of course there were cats!), a responsibility that entailed my being allowed to enter Crystal's domain at will. I intended to take full advantage of this privilege. I would search every nook and cranny for evidence of drug use, pornography, exotic methods of contraception (I'd know it when I saw it), treatments for rare, sexually related afflictions, and, of course, any hint of Eric's fate. In fact I confined myself more or less to what was in plain view, fearing that major disarrangement might be noticed, though the medicine cabinet and certain dresser drawers received careful attention.

But all was, as I should have been able to predict, blandness. No trace of anything other than a life lived in a vacuum, or at best, an antiseptic cocoon.

I was religious about my duties as feeder of cats.

Crystal came back at midnight on a weekend, a warm rain falling steadily. At last it was possible to believe that things could grow in this place. Would I care to come up and join her for a nightcap of duty-free Drambuie? Yes. Yes, I would. So began our second—and so far last—conversation.

We sat on her living room floor. Why we did this I can no longer remember. She put on a CD, not Kate Bush thank God but some male vocalist unknown to me, the repugnant sound one associates with the phrase "easy listening." Crystal began to talk about men, her inability to find one who was worthy of her. (She could offer plenty of examples from her holiday.) I was pleased that she seemed ready to enter a territory of frankness she had walked briskly past in our conversational encounter in the fall.

Men. Don't get her started. (Actually, I hadn't.) The mechanics from her father's dealership where she had been a secretary the previous summer. She had, she said "worked her way through" most of them. She sounded sad. There was a lawyer her parents wanted to set her up with, but the very thought of him made her want to retch.

Crystal, Crystal, I thought. Mechanics! Lawyers! Men whose professional lives are based on grease and lies, respectively. Of course there is occasion for sadness here. How right you are to feel it, to articulate it. How fortunate you are, too, to know someone who understands, someone who can help you confront the situation, these Gilmore-like mechanics, these Bundyesque lawyers.

But I said nothing, preferring that Crystal come to such realizations on her own. As she continued to speak, more softly now it seemed, I leaned over (all the better to hear her) and found my face disappearing into her soft blond hair, disappearing in the sense that it no longer functioned as face (utilitarian, unprepossessing) but rather as an organ of sensuousness exploring this blond plenitude whose texture mysteriously invited playful disintegration of self, joyous merging with otherness. And then inevitably we were kissing, my tongue sliding confidently into her mouth, the first time since moving to that city that any part of my body had penetrated the fleshly perimeter of another living being.

And then—and of course one should have foreseen this— everything changed. I felt the firm clasp of her perfect teeth, immobilizing my tongue with impersonal precision. There appeared to be no attempt to inflict pain, only to demonstrate control. Experimental wiggling revealed that neither advance nor retreat was for the moment possible. Crystal's eyes remained closed; an observer might have inferred bliss.

And it came to me that Crystal, the real Crystal, was not really in control, that her body was reacting as it had been programmed to, that a lifetime of socialization had caused to accept certain negative generalizations about men, and that, oddly, she had failed to notice that I was an exception to them. And I now felt certain about Eric's fate. Eric was no murderer. Eric, I now saw clearly, had *been* murdered by the same ruthless defence system that had somehow just been triggered, his body disposed of in some ingenious manner gleaned from criminology textbooks, perhaps to be used as fertilizer for this year's lawn and flowerbeds.

Then the teeth released their grip. Freed, my tongue insisted on one final playful flick before withdrawing—as though to proclaim that it had not been humiliated but rather had merely done the frivolous thing it had set out to do, no hard feelings, right?

Eric returned from the land of the dead to enter the more comforting realm of the moved-on-somewhere-else.

It was, remarkably, as though nothing had happened. The Drambuie gradually disappeared. Then it was daylight.

• • •

And so, Crystal, we return to the present, this summer moment as I contemplate your mother's remark about flower heaven. And I recall your desire to know about how the other half lives (expressed so forlornly in your brief career as a cocktail waitress) and understand it as an attempt to evade the destiny that the world and your mother have designed for you. Crystal, you were not meant to have sex with mechanics and marry lawyers.

The other half, Crystal, the other half does not live in flower heaven.

Soon I will be giving notice. My contract has not been renewed. The pink-haired supervisor's successor has realized that I hate young people. Yesterday he called me into his office and prefaced our dialogue with the following accusation: "You're not a happy camper, are you?" Like Eric before me, I will be moving on. The next inhabitant of your basement will know nothing of your nearly imperceptible sorrow, your instinctive and so far futile combat with the strangely benign-looking gigantic amoeba that is blandness. And you will, I fear, slowly become more like your mother, even more, one might say, for it might as well have been your mother's teeth on my tongue that spring night, those teeth giving fair warning that one's manhood might be cruelly and suddenly uprooted.

How naive of me to think that the language of the flesh might speak with the honesty and clarity that I know you deserve. Instead, in the end, I have only this.

The voice whispering in your head, Crystal, the one your mother denies when she speaks mockingly of flower heaven, the voice that comes from deep within the foundations of your house (your mother's house!), the voice that would shake those foundations with its calm words of enlightenment, the voice of unprepossession, that voice, Crystal, is mine.

THE FJORD

t's Vancouver, the eighties are about to begin, it's early summer, and Hanrahan has hit rock bottom. He's decided to drop out of grad school. He's done nothing on his dissertation for months. He's lost the energy, the vision, if he ever had them. How could he ever have had them? Wordsworth's sonnets—a topic so trivial that no one has bothered to take it seriously before Hanrahan, or at least, Hanrahan's supervisor. A lost cause. Hanrahan has no job, nor any serious prospect of getting one. He's broke. His girlfriend, Sharon, is all he has, and she's starting to bail on him. She's completed her own dissertation, believes passionately in its importance, and is now busily turning it into a book, even as she teaches a full course load as a sessional. She doesn't quite understand what's happened to the Hanrahan she began living with a little less than a year ago. Neither does he.

Not that he hasn't tried. Lately he's had three interviews for community college jobs. But he never gets an offer. The most recent one was held in a suite in a downtown hotel, two men, one in a business suit (the dean of something) and the other, bearded, in jeans, workboots, and a plaid workshirt, on the college's board as a representative of the community, in a remote part of the province Hanrahan had never heard of before seeing the advertisement for the job.

The dean began by saying, "Folks up where we're from *hate* books. I don't mean they're indifferent to them or that they mildly dislike them; they actively *loathe* the very *idea* of reading. Tell us how you'd attempt to be an effective teacher in that sort of environment."

Hanrahan can no longer remember what he said in reply. Then the bearded one said, "Our town is pretty much your average small town, I guess. Half the people are drunks and the other half are fundamentalist Christians. How do you think you'd like living up there?"

Hanrahan has forgotten his reply to this one, too. In fact, he's forgotten everything that happened after that, except that they said they'd be in touch with him within a week if they were going to offer him the job, and more than a week has now passed, and he's heard nothing. Even Sharon, chronically optimistic, has begun to lose hope. And now, of course, she's turning on him.

"Hanrahan," she's saying, "it's time you got a job. I don't mean a teaching job, I mean *any* kind of job. I don't care what, minimum wage or whatever. It's time you started contributing something around here."

There is some justice in her complaint, Hanrahan acknowledges. She's paid the rent herself for the last however many months. (Is it two? Three? Four? Surely not.) Hanrahan has sort of given up trying to keep track. And then there's food. Several times a week she makes entries in a scribbler, delineating in excruciating detail how much she has spent and how little Hanrahan has. So yes, she does have a point. A very good one.

But Hanrahan's options are limited. How do you find a job? He's not from Vancouver, and neither is Sharon, so there's no network of hometown contacts to draw on. Almost all the people they know, they've met at the university, and most of them are from elsewhere, too. But then Hanrahan thinks of Dave Summerall, a local boy who's been helpful to him in the past. It was Dave who helped Hanrahan get his summer job last year, teaching at the Special Programs division of a local community college. Of course there's no chance of his getting that job back. Special Programs, through its director of instruction, a Ms. Genevieve Butterfield, has made it clear that, on balance, it would be best if Hanrahan were to evaporate from its collective memory. Hanrahan attributes this attitude to an injudicious remark he made to her about one of the administrators at the main campus, a man named Wade. Hanrahan was unaware that despite the difference in their surnames, Ms. Butterfield and Wade…

In any case, Dave said at the time that he felt responsible for the whole thing, that he should have warned Hanrahan about

Butterfield-Wade. Dave is of course back at Special Programs this summer, staking out territory for a permanent job. But Hanrahan remembers that Dave once ran down a list of a dozen or so jobs he's had in the recent past—gas station attendant, waiter, clerk in a bookstore, desk clerk, labourer, proofreader, and so on. Innumerable contacts. And he's on the record as feeling bad about what happened last year, Hanrahan thinks gleefully as he dials.

Twenty-four hours later Hanrahan has a job. He's a desk clerk at a motel. Actually, it calls itself a "motor hotel"—it's in the West End, less than a block from English Bay, close to the park. The Fjord Motor Hotel. Dave, who used to work there himself, has kept in touch with the owner, a Greek guy named Charlie. Charlie is always on the lookout for desk clerks who are reliable, at least semi-literate, and willing to work for very little more than the minimum wage. Hanrahan is one of the few people on the Lower Mainland who qualifies on all three counts.

There's nothing to the job. Hanrahan's shift is from four to midnight. He checks people in. He works the switchboard. He chats with people passing through the tiny lobby. That's almost it. There are about forty rooms on three floors, and the place is filled, most nights—mostly with tourists, though there's always a rock band or two (Charlie has some arrangement with a couple of nightclubs) and about half a dozen prostitutes who show up regularly.

There's an adjoining restaurant, run by Charlie's brother, Pete. Half an hour into his first shift, Hanrahan faces the first major test of his desk-clerking career. Pete comes in from the restaurant, waving a fistful of bills. "Give me a fifty," he says. Hanrahan gives it to him, takes the smaller bills in return. "You gave me six tens." A contemptuous smirk crosses Pete's face: "Ah, you are honest." Charlie, who's been watching discreetly from the doorway to the restaurant, nods and walks away. Hanrahan is on board.

Later that week Hanrahan pulls off his first business coup. It's a quarter to twelve. The motel is full. A prostitute comes in with a client, a Japanese tourist. Hanrahan knows she's one of the regulars, but also knows she's somehow different from the others. Susan, her name is. She's beautiful, but then so are some of the others. What makes her different? Well, Hanrahan doesn't like the word, but it's the sense of *innocence* that she projects. She doesn't have the hard eyes, the coarse sense of humour, the rote flirtatiousness of body language that Hanrahan has already realized are the infallible marks. Or doesn't have those things yet, he reminds himself. Let's not get carried away, H. But for now. Tall, dark-haired, Susan looks like the Queen of the Prom, a teenager's notion of the ideal date. Here she is, speaking with what to Hanrahan seems to be real tenderness to her client, who probably doesn't understand more than ten per cent of what she's saying.

Hanrahan has explained that there's no room at the inn. Susan looks sad, as if her puppy has wandered off God knows where more than half an hour ago now. "We could go to my place, I guess," she says, doubtfully, to her client, who nods frantically and grins at her and at Hanrahan by turns. She knows all the hotels around here will be full, she says, pouting slightly.

Inspiration strikes Hanrahan. There's a back room where Charlie stores supplies. Milton, the night man, keeps a cot back there for the dead time between two and six when nothing happens. Hanrahan explains all this. He'd charge only half the usual price of a room. Susan's eyes light up, full of gratitude, Hanrahan imagines. Perhaps he has a friend for life. Or not. He shows them the way.

At midnight Milton shows up. He and his wife, Jean, are the only permanent residents of the Fjord. Milton is a tall middle-aged nearly-bald Englishman. He's a Christian Scientist, a fact which to Hanrahan connotes a vague sense of probably harmless wackiness. Milton is annoyingly suspicious of people of colour ("they're not wanted"; by whom? Hanrahan wants to ask but doesn't). He makes a few extra bucks by perpetrating horrendous black velvet paintings, examples of which are always on display in the lobby. Once a serious-looking man in a suit came in off the street and asked Hanrahan who the artist was. Hanrahan said he didn't know. Not his job to promote bad taste.

But that's in the future. Now Hanrahan explains why the door to the back room is now shut. Milton thinks about this for a moment. Then he speaks, oddly solemn: "Charlie will be pleased." The words shower over Hanrahan like a blessing

Soon he's become a fixture at the Fjord. A fixture. Ponder that, Hanrahan. (And why is the Fjord called the Fjord? No one knows. Were the original owners, or the owners from whom Charlie bought the place Norwegian, perhaps? No, Milton says, Chinese. He thinks the surname may have been Nee.) After two weeks, Hanrahan has been there forever. From four to midnight, he runs the show. Not that there's that much to run. In fact, he spends most of his time waiting for something to happen, and when it does, it's entirely trivial, the phone ringing, a guest asking about something on the way out, someone looking for a pay phone or a public washroom with a condom dispenser (sorry), or directions to Stanley Park. Further, it's impossible for Hanrahan to concentrate on anything else, reading a book, for example— you just get started, and there's another interruption.

Yet—and here's the odd part—he rather enjoys this job. Nobody here asks how his thesis is going. No one asks about his prospects of getting a teaching job. No one ever wonders how things are between him and Sharon. For eight hours a day, his so-called real life is on hold. He can relax. How does he pass the time? Well, embarrassing to relate, he eavesdrops on people's telephone conversations. During the course of his employment at the Fjord, he learns a great deal about relationships, Black slang, loneliness, the street price of various recreational drugs, despair, what people say to each other when they have nothing to say.

And he'll talk with anyone who passes through the lobby. It's amazing what people will say to desk clerks. He hears more than one life story as he perches on his stool behind the desk, a secular priest with no power of absolution.

But of course he still has plenty of time to himself, plenty of time to think. About what? Well, there's the morass into which his academic career has fallen, but that's not a major long-term concern. Hanrahan is of the right age and class to know that, sooner or later, the right job will come along, at more or less the right money. Hanrahan's is perhaps the last generation of Canadians to be able to luxuriate in this belief, and he's always taken full advantage of that privilege.

On the other hand, there's question of him and Sharon, the long-term question there. That's a killer.

Sharon wants to marry him. He doesn't particularly want to marry her. Why not? No concise, credible answer to that one is currently available. And she's starting to put on some pressure—not just the predictable biological clock stuff (neither of them is yet within hailing distance of thirty, so he can't take that seriously), but other, more sinister measures. For example. Recently she's gone off the pill and replaced it with a foul, medicinal-smelling foam. Hanrahan is sure that she's done this to punish him, despite her protestations to the contrary: "I've been on the pill since I was seventeen, Hanrahan. It's not good for me to stay on it any longer." And so on. Well, Hanrahan asked, couldn't she at least get a foam that comes in different scents—orange, maybe, or lemon, or even chocolate would… "I am not," Sharon interrupted sternly, "a candy store."

But back to the main issue. *Why* doesn't he want to marry her? The question arises, explicitly, in his second week at the Fjord, during a conversation with Jean, Milton's wife. Jean often comes down to chat with Hanrahan, especially late in the evening, just before Milton's own shift is about to start. Milton apparently likes to have time to himself as he prepares to meet his public.

So Jean will come down to the lobby around eleven-thirty to sit in the black shiny armchair nearest the desk.

Unfortunately she looks a bit like Shelley Winters. She has a sweet maternal side to her, the sweetness stemming perhaps from the fact that she's never had kids of her own—one of her first confidences. She does her mothering on her chihuahua and on Milton, in that order.

"He's a strange man," she tells Hanrahan, "but I've never loved anyone so deeply in my life."

Poor woman, Hanrahan thinks. He's seen sad cases before, but never a middle-aged racist Christian Scientist who can't get a better job than night desk clerk at the Fjord, and who, to top it off, does paintings on black velvet.

In any case, that's Milton, Jean and Milton, the Fjord's answer to *Love Story*. Don't be snotty, Hanrahan. And then Jean is asking *him* about his relationship with Sharon, and he's hard pressed to come up with good answers.

"But Sugar," Jean says, "if *she* wants to be with *you*, and *you* want to be with *her*, and neither of you is married to anybody else, what's the problem?"

"It's hard to explain," Hanrahan replies. And certainly there are all sorts of good reasons to marry. Sharon's character, for one: stability, reliability, integrity. Honesty. She'll tell you exactly what she thinks, about everything. She's the only person Hanrahan has ever met who's like this, and he's coming to the conclusion that probably to meet one such person in a lifetime is beating the odds. Of course this means that his ego takes a whipping in their daily life together, but Hanrahan has enough residual Catholicism in him to believe that this is for the best.

If that's a downside, it's a minor one. Hanrahan can handle that sort of thing. So far we have one good reason *for*, and none *against*.

Is it that Sharon isn't attractive enough for him, or not exciting enough in bed? No, and no. The problem does not lie in this area at all. Not that Sharon's a knockout or anything, but that's never been an issue with Hanrahan, who is himself nothing to write home about. So unobsessed is he with Sharon's looks that he has difficulty describing her to others. Her eyes are brown, he's sure of that, and her hair is sort of brown (though the colour changes in ways he can't quite explain, depending on the light and the time of year), and as for her face, well how *do* you describe someone's face, someone, that is, who doesn't resemble somebody famous, or some member of the animal kingdom? So Sharon is not horse-faced, and she wouldn't remind you of your favourite female movie star—do you have a problem with that? In any case, Jean, Hanrahan has her picture in his wallet. Here. He'll show you.

("Gorgeous," Jean says with profound insincerity. "Why, she's absolutely gorgeous.")

Okay, sex. Hanrahan does not discuss this with Jean, or with anyone else. But in a sense there's nothing to discuss. It's not a problem. He and Sharon are well-matched, as far as energy and enthusiasm are concerned. They don't share the more exotic tastes of some of Sharon's girlfriends, who are forever regaling her with accounts of bizarre positions, action, locations, combinations. After one such call, Sharon asks Hanrahan anxiously whether he minds that they're not like Duncan and Angela.

"What do you mean?"

"Well, right now they're probably having sex while hanging by their toes from the chandelier."

"I didn't know they had a chandelier."

"They don't, but you know what I mean."

"No, I don't mind."

"Good."

And of course honesty permeates the bedroom. "I will not, under any circumstances, fake orgasm," Sharon announced after one of their first times together.

"Great. Neither will I."

Yes, there's no lack of communication here. Well, if Hanrahan is happy with Sharon, is it that Sharon is not, herself, enough? Does he simply want a variety of sexual partners? No, he doesn't think so. In his life Hanrahan has been with perhaps ten or a dozen women, well below average for someone of his age and generation, he imagines. Several of these women appeared and quickly disappeared in the immediate pre-Sharon period. A disquieting percentage were women about whom Hanrahan thought, on first meeting them: "No, not this one. Not ever. Not under any circumstances." And then, a few weeks, or days, or even hours later, there they'd be in a bedroom ripping each other's clothes off. Well, not literally, but still. No, Hanrahan does not want to go back to that. Monogamy holds no terrors for him.

What *is* your problem, then, Hanrahan? Well, we don't have to figure it out all at once. Life at the Fjord offers its occasional distractions. For example: Hanrahan's one and only encounter with a Living Blues Legend.

Most of the bands that stay at the motel are composed of non-entities, kids on the way up (or so they probably think) or slightly older musicians who aren't going any higher: Sweet Taste of Sin, specializing in Milwaukee blues, whatever that is; The Caramel Vacuum, anemic-looking blond guys from California struggling to look like surfers; Shorty Poindexter and the Raindrops, soul music from the cotton fields outside Seattle. Some have slightly higher profiles, the New York Babes, for example. (Trouble here with one of the chambermaids, who refuses to change the linen on the bed of a man who wears a blouse.) Early one evening, the Babes phone out to an industrial supply company to have some oxygen sent over. (Hanrahan monitors the call.) A minute later he receives one himself, from the manager of the company. "Who are these guys? Do they have a legitimate reason for purchasing oxygen?"

"No, they just want to get high. They're musicians, bums."

That about sums up Hanrahan's attitude to the bands. But the Living Blues Legend is an exception. He's right up there with Muddy Waters, Lightnin' Hopkins, people like that. It's sad, Hanrahan thinks, to see him reduced to playing at a club that uses the Fjord. And that's not the half of it. Travelling with the band is his son, Junior, who's about seventeen, Hanrahan guesses. He's never seen anyone so strung out. Junior is a skinny kid whose limbs jerk unpredictably; he staggers when he walks, and he talks too fast for Hanrahan and most other people to understand him well. Then there's his facial twitch. And the fact that he's constantly begging for money.

"Gimme five," he'll say, lurching across the lobby at the desk.

"What?"

"Gimme five dollars. A lend of five dollars."

"No."

"Here." And Junior slaps down a handful of change on the desk, maybe $1.25 worth.

"Take this out of two."

"What?"

"Take this out of two. Gimme two dollars and take the change."

"Why?" And here Junior stares at Hanrahan uncomprehendingly, as if any sentient being should appreciate the justice of the proposed exchange.

"Shee-it" says Junior, with contempt, staggering toward elevator, dropping dimes and quarters as he goes.

One day misfortune strikes. Junior, stoned, steals a car, is involved in a minor accident about two blocks from the Fjord, and flees the scene.

When Hanrahan comes on shift at four, he's brought up to speed by Joanne, who does the eight-to-four shift.

"He's hiding in his room," Joanne says. "The band is out somewhere. It's only a matter of time before the cops show up. They know who he is. Apparently he made sure that people at the scene knew whose son he is."

And show up the cops do, less than half an hour later, asking for the key to Junior's room, the better to surprise him, dangerous criminal that he is. Hanrahan obeys Charlie's standing order: "Give the police whatever they want. Don't even ask questions." (The police, of course, know that a certain percentage of Charlie's income derives from his knowingly renting rooms to prostitutes; Charlie had better co-operate with them.) And so the police drag Junior away. He doesn't go quietly, either.

An hour later, Hanrahan looks up from some paperwork to see the Living Blues Legend himself on the other side of the desk. He's wearing a cowboy hat. Unending pain reflected on the aged, ageless face. Nobody knows the trouble he's seen, Hanrahan thinks. (And rebukes himself while thinking it—what a mindlessly white-liberal thing to be thinking.)

"Did the po-lice come for Junior?"

"Yes, they did."

"Did the po-lice take Junior away?"

"Yes, they did."

Hanrahan feels as if he's driven nails into the palms of the Living Blues Legend.

"Thank you, son."

And he turns away. Something about the use of the word "son" touches Hanrahan, makes him feel even sadder. He glares at three members of the Caramel Vacuum, who have been snickering over by the door.

"Do you guys want to pay for that long-distance call to San

Jose last night?" Charlie's markup policy on long-distance is fifteen per cent. Hanrahan adds twenty-five.

And later he thinks, maybe that's why I don't want to marry Sharon, to deal myself in to that sinister lifelong family game of hurting and being hurt. Maybe I'm just scared to death of that.

But that can't be the whole story, he thinks. There must be more to it. And as, over the next few evenings, he uses his dead time at the Fjord to ponder the issue, another idea begins to make its presence known. It lumbers like some prehistoric beast from the periphery of his consciousness toward the clean, well-lighted place in his mind where Hanrahan can finally begin to take photographs, conduct experiments, draw reasoned conclusions. It is, Hanrahan comes to believe, the real reason that he doesn't want to marry Sharon.

It's sort of embarrassing, actually. Hanrahan has never been in love.

Well, that's not quite true. Hanrahan was in love once, for a whole year, when he was fifteen. The girl in question never discovered this. Hanrahan was too shy to approach her, except for purposes of casual conversation. But this didn't matter. For Hanrahan the experience was complete, perfect, even without her conscious participation. It is, he thinks, the most important relationship in his life to date. While he regrets that it was the sort of relationship that didn't directly involve another person, it is nevertheless the benchmark against which he measures all others. What has remained with Hanrahan for the years since it happened is the way in which his knowledge of the girl's

presence in the world enriched his life for an entire year. (After
which point her influence faded gently away, and Hanrahan, his
year of solitary paradise expired, returned to the fallen world of
normal mid-adolescence.)

Looking back from the perspective of the Fjord, Hanrahan,
who has by now imbibed the obligatory dosages of Freud, Jung
and others, has all sorts of theories about the meaning of the
experience. But the fact remains that nothing he has known since
has come close to it, for emotional power, depth, authenticity.

If he loves Sharon, it is not "love" in this sense. But Hanrahan
wishes it were. Realizing that this is true of course resolves nothing. In fact, it poses new problems. Can he talk to Sharon about
it? Is so, how? And what is the honourable thing to do in these
circumstances—break off with Sharon and go on seeking true
love until he finds it? Or forget about his adolescent dream and
reconcile himself to the quite palatable situation that fate seems
to have designed for him?

For the moment, Hanrahan decides to adopt a traditional
strategy: let things ride for a while.

In the meantime, he's making considerably more money at
the Fjord than he'd anticipated, thanks to Susan, with whom he
has, in a sense, become partners. It works this way. Susan will
bring a client to the hotel at some point fairly early in the evening. In less than an hour, usually much less, the john will clear
out, making a beeline to the door without so much as a glance
in Hanrahan's direction. A few minutes later Susan will show
up, looking, as always, immaculate, usually with a big smile for

Hanrahan, who will already have called a cab for her. Susan is not one to waste time while on duty. She wants to go back to wherever she goes to pick up her clients as soon as possible—much as she would like, she intimates from time to time, to enjoy a long private conversation with Hanrahan. Before coming down to the lobby, Susan will have changed the sheets using spare linen that Hanrahan has placed there earlier in his shift. When she comes back with another man, usually within an hour, but certainly before Hanrahan goes off shift at midnight, he will rent the new client the same room. Later he and Susan will split the money fifty-fifty. No one need be the wiser. And sometimes, if the stars align, they can do the same deal with a third client.

This doesn't happen every night, but it happens often enough to increase Hanrahan's take-home pay a noticeable amount. Sometimes he wonders about his business relationship with Susan. His initial sense that she is somehow different from the others has not altered. Unfailingly, she conjures up images of the Homecoming Queen, the Girl Next Door, healthy, innocent, clean-cut beauty. What is she like when she's not working? Hanrahan is free to speculate. Does she have *real* lovers? He knows better than to ask.

During the afternoon and evening of the night on which Hanrahan finally asks Sharon to marry him, the following events occur.

When Hanrahan comes on shift at four, Joanne tells him there may be a problem with one of the guests, a Mr. Jeffries from Nanaimo, maybe Hanrahan remembered him, a tall man in his fifties? Anyway, he's been in his room all day, won't answer the phone or respond to knocks on the door. Last seen by Milton, at about one in the morning. Charlie's policy on such matters is to call the police in, after a sufficient amount of time has elapsed, which it now has. See you, Hanrahan.

Pete, from the restaurant, has been hovering in the background during this discussion. He is, Hanrahan has by now realized, a real lightweight, the kid brother given the job at which he can do least harm. Now there is about him the air of a schoolboy who's been given the day off.

"He could be dead," he tells Hanrahan, an eight-year-old imparting implausible information about sex.

Hanrahan calls the cops.

In due course, a cop appears, the old-fashioned red-faced kind who will invariably squint in hatred at Hanrahan for no reason he has ever been able to discern. Asshole, Hanrahan thinks at him, from behind his mask of professional serenity.

He explains the situation. The cop reluctantly takes the passkey. "You wanna come up?" Apparently it's a matter of protocol (or possibly even law?) that an employee be present. Hanrahan is torn. From the way both Pete and the cop are acting, it's pretty obvious that the guy must be dead. Hanrahan has never seen a corpse, and there is, he finds, an unexpected epicentre of curiosity sending minor shockwaves through his brain. On the other hand, he has a duty here. There are rooms to rent, and potential customers wandering in off the street, seeing a desk with no desk clerk behind it, may wander out again.

"It's okay, I'll go," Pete says. They go. Hanrahan stares absently out the window. No one wanders in off the street. They come back. "He's dead," Pete says, quietly triumphant, having been proved right about something. The cop gives Hanrahan a number to call to get the right people to come to take the corpse away. "Looks like a heart attack," he says.

The corpse professionals come and do their job. They whisk it through the lobby, covered in a grey blanket, upright, strapped on a stretcher, and are gone before Hanrahan can say thanks. A few minutes later one of Shorty Poindexter's Raindrops races from the elevator, eyes bulging.

"Was a man killed in this hotel? Was he shot? Was it murder?"

"No, no," Hanrahan says. "This is Canada. We don't shoot people in hotels. He died of natural causes. It's all perfectly natural."

Pete comes back from the restaurant. "Are you going to rent that room again tonight?" The tone is odd, as if he's suggesting that they should commit a minor crime together, for kicks.

No, Hanrahan decides, that room will not be rented tonight. In honour of the dead. Executive decision. Pete does not object. Hanrahan is in charge, master of the Fjord. As he's thinking this, the image of a real fjord appears in his mind's eye, Hanrahan navigating his small craft between ever-narrowing cliffs, moving deeper into a continent, no doubt toward some archetypal dead end.

In the early evening, earlier than usual, Susan comes in. There's another young woman with her, one Hanrahan has never seen before, but cut from the same cloth, tall, elegant, high cheekbones like Susan's but ash blond hair instead of dark, the only obvious difference that Hanrahan registers at first glance.

"This is Elaine," Susan says. "She'll be coming in fairly regularly now. This is Hanrahan. He's cool."

Yes, Hanrahan thinks, I suppose I am cool, in the sense she means it. Is that something to celebrate?

"Elaine will be back later tonight. Save her a room, okay? It's her first time."

"With pleasure."

They disappear. Her first time. Hanrahan, predictably, feels sad about this. Come off it, Hanrahan. Why should you? We're not talking about exploitation here. Look around the lobby. Do you see any Black pimps flashing handguns? Elaine's eyes are bright and clear. No pathetic drug-glazed zombie stuff. Intelligent young women making rational career choices, that's all it is.

It's not quite dark when Elaine comes back, with a tall man in his fifties, a man, Hanrahan thinks, who corresponds to Joanne's description of Mr. Jeffries. (In the meantime Mrs. Jeffries has phoned, seeking details, which Hanrahan of course has been unable to supply. He has found himself referring to Mr. Jeffries as having "passed away," hating himself as he uttered the phrase.) In any case, here's someone who could well have been Jeffries, the first client of Elaine's career. There's irony for you.

He signs the card as "Smith." "Very original, sir," Hanrahan says. Sometimes johns like this sort of banter, man-to-man bull-shit. Mr. Smith merely blinks and looks confused. Elaine leads him toward the elevator.

About half an hour later the phone rings. It's Susan, wanting to be connected to Elaine's room. Hanrahan of course decides to listen in. Oboyoboyoboy, he thinks. What does the first whore say to the second whore? This is going to be good.

"Are you okay?" Susan is saying.

"Yeah, we're doing fine," Elaine says.

"I just wanted to make sure that, you know, everything is going well."

"We're doing fine. We'll be finishing up soon. Everything is great."

"Okay, good. See you later. Take care." They hang up. Take care? That's *it*? What a disappointment. Well, Hanrahan, what were you expecting? Oh, inside technical whore talk with a high overt filth quotient. Since you're asking. Shame on you, Hanrahan. Yes, I know.

Soon Elaine and Mr. Smith are history, at least for the evening. Elaine flashes a perfect Susan-like smile at Hanrahan as she leaves.

Shortly after eleven, Jean comes down to chat. Somehow she gets on the subject of religion, more specifically her baptism by total immersion in some outdoor swimming pool in Tennessee when she was seventeen. "It was a warm summer night. I was wearing a white robe over my bathing suit, we all did. The preacher wore hip waders, Reverend Hufnagel, his name was. He'd sort of pull you over backwards. I could see the stars just before I went under. It was beautiful."

At this moment a strange shape staggers in from the street. It's about four and a half feet tall, and it's making a noise that seems to be a hybrid of a snarl and a grunt. It collapses in a heap mid-lobby, limbs thrashing, the noises continuing, somewhat muted.

Only then does Hanrahan recognize the figure as human. It's a man, one he's seen before. To get home after his shift, Hanrahan has to take two buses. His transfer point is a stop outside a seedy hotel up on Granville, much farther downscale than the Fjord ever dreamed of being. During the ten minutes or so that he normally has to wait, he has seen this man often, lurching out of one door of the hotel and back in through another, wearing a white jacket of the sort that waiters might wear, often carrying, incongruously enough, a wicker basket on his arm; whatever was in the basket would be concealed by linen napkins.

He's obviously drunk now.

Hanrahan remembers all this in the time it takes for Jean to say "Dear Lord Jesus."

The man on the floor is extremely ugly, Hanrahan remembers (though he can't see the ugliness clearly at the moment). Mouth set partly open in an odd expression that seemed to connote either disdainful amusement or agony. Viewed from Hanrahan's angle, the man's head looks like Sluggo's in the *Nancy* comic strip, a perfect circle with little black dots.

Jean is bending over him, solicitous. "The poor man absolutely *reeks* of alcohol."

"Shall I call the police?"

"Shoot, no, I'll deal with him. I know where he lives."

Somehow this does not surprise Hanrahan.

"Can I help you with him?"

"No, honey, stay right there."

She drags him to his feet. He starts making different noises now, possibly indicating that he recognizes Jean, a sort of whimpering. He leans against her as she whisks him around the corner, out of Hanrahan's sight.

She's back in ten minutes, flushed, grinning. "Little bugger tried to seduce me," she says, admiringly. "I had one hell of a time getting away from him."

Later, as he walks the block and a half to the bus stop, it comes to Hanrahan that this will be the night that he will ask Sharon to marry him, and she of course will say Yes. And that will be that.

HANRAHAN
AGONISTES

The eighties have arrived and here's Hanrahan in Calgary, a
city where he knows no one and which he already hates.
He can't breathe the air, for one thing. It's too dry. Also
the wind blows all the time, turning early September into late
November in a heartbeat.

Why is he here? A job, of course. Not the tenure-track gravy
train that lurched off the trestle about a decade ago, when, in
the twinkling of an eye (whose eye?), it seemed that suddenly
there were no tenure-track jobs available in Canadian universities
anymore, the system having expanded rapidly in the sixties in
preparation for the first wave of kids born just after the war. And
Hanrahan, wouldn't you know it, didn't notice until it was too late.
The real jobs, when they anomalously appeared (an untimely
faculty death, perhaps) would go to the elite, people, in fact,

like his fiancée, Sharon, of whom more in a moment. Hanrahan had intended to drop out (to do what?), but after so many years couldn't bring himself to do it, needing, perhaps, to tell himself that one day things would change, he'd finish his dissertation, on hold for at least five years now, he'd get it published, somehow he'd beat the odds... and so on. So here he was, hanging in, on the outermost fringes of academe, newly employed but in a temporary, menial sort of job—at the university, yes, that will look okay on the CV, but teaching remedial writing, a fact that may turn out to be, as people are beginning to say now, problematic.

He's left Sharon behind, in Vancouver, though that's hardly the way to put it. Sharon is in place, in Vancouver, completing her dissertation, up to her eyeballs in fellowship money, compiling (he guesses is the word) a strong publication record. As gases ejected from the sun once congealed into comparatively tiny planets, so Hanrahan has been spun off by Sharon, sent forth to travel the dusty byways to become, insofar as he is capable of it, self-supporting, for a change. It is understood that in a year or so they will marry, when Sharon "completes"—a verb that, in their conversation, indecently lacks quotation marks and never needs a direct object. Hanrahan knows that he himself will never "complete," will in all probability never *be* complete. He and Sharon have arrived at a tacit understanding about this, one not extended to Hanrahan's supervisor, who has for some months now been awaiting the next (second) chapter of "Wordsworth's Sonnets: Myth, Ritual, Archetype," an academic project so cynically conceived that Hanrahan is at times in awe of his own good fortune in having gotten away with it so far. (But what, really has he gotten away with? Well, he's still in the doctoral program, isn't he? Yes, and just try taking that to the bank and see how much they'll loan you.) But he also feels something like guilt. There is that tiny shard of what he'd prefer not to call integrity buried somewhere, several levels down in the ruined city of his consciousness—like Schliemann's Troy, go down far enough and who knows what you'll find.

And speaking of antitheses, here's Calgary, a city of spanking new surfaces with nothing human underneath it (he imagines) but the sewer system. Calgary, city of self-righteously full employment, of impeccably kept lawns, of everything-paved-over-where-possible. Hanrahan has yet to see a saunterer, let alone a lounger or identifiable layabout. City that is not Vancouver.

No life would be possible here. Life is in the past (with Sharon) or in the future (with Sharon). There is no present.

• • •

All incoming first-year students are required to write an essay on a topic of general interest. The significant percentage who fail will be required to take the non-credit course taught by Hanrahan and about a dozen other career-challenged instructors. The students will resent this mightily but will not be allowed to graduate until they have passed the course. The instructors will use a textbook that has chapters on comma splices and dangling modifiers. They will move through it in lockstep, supervised by a certifiable madman, Dr. Rex Bindle, seconded from the

English Department, the onlie begetter of the remedial program, a narcissistic ectomorph who seems perpetually about to spring up on his toes and sometimes does (thus increasing his height to about six foot six), while peering down at his target, the sort of gesture that is the equivalent of saying, "I'm taller than you and therefore superior in all other respects as well. What do you think of that, short person?"

When Hanrahan entered his office for the first time, Bindle peered at him for a moment, having been forewarned of his arrival, and said, simply, "Boffo!"

"I beg your pardon?"

"Boffo. The word 'boffo.' Do you think it reasonable or unreasonable for a graduate of the Alberta secondary system to be familiar with the word 'boffo'?"

Hanrahan's not dumb. In his world, trashing high schools is always a safe bet.

"Reasonable, I would say." (The "I would say" a self-conscious addition to impress on Bindle his, Hanrahan's scholarly thoughtfulness in such matters.)

"Reasonable! Of course!" Bindle barked. "Of course it's reasonable."

Some years before, on the very first writing competency test ever given, students were required to read a brief newspaper article and write an essay in response to it. The word "boffo" appeared in the article. A public controversy ensued. The local paper, in a closely reasoned editorial, concluded that "boffo" was unfairly exotic, given the context.

"But then," Bindle went on, enthusiastically, "not four months later, there was *this*." He sprang up and gestured frantically at a bulletin board on the wall behind him. "You see? You see?" He extracted a piece of newspaper from the board and thrust it at Hanrahan. "Just the headline, that's all you need."

The headline included the word "boffo."

"There it is! The forbidden word. The word Albertans must be shielded from at all cost! In big bold print in their own pathetic rag. Hah-hah! Boffo indeed!"

Hanrahan attempted to express, by the way he held the paper, an attitude of academic detachment. He nodded judiciously.

"That's what we're up against, Mr. Hanrahan. That's what Alberta is all about!"

• • •

Hanrahan has a one-bedroom furnished apartment with a small balcony that overlooks a parking lot and a strip mall. Next door is a house with a backyard where a cocker spaniel tied to the clothesline barks all day long. Hanrahan almost never sees his fellow tenants, though there's about a dozen other apartments in the building. Occasionally he catches a glimpse of someone disappearing around a corner or closing a door. Perhaps the place is haunted, he thinks for a moment before acknowledging that the banality of the situation—the building, the city, his new death-in-life—would hardly allow for anything so unusual. How could there be ghosts where there has (as far as Hanrahan knows) been no life.

• • •

Hanrahan takes particular note of three of his female colleagues. There's Dr. Bindle's wife, Amelia, a sour-looking woman in her late forties (and thus older than Bindle) but in other ways conventionally matched with him: an American Gothic-style elongated face and body that radiate emotional desiccation. Amelia is, her manner declares immediately to Hanrahan, intellectually superior to him on grounds that he need not attempt to establish. As far as degrees and other tangible achievements are concerned, well, she's sacrificed her career for her husband's, hasn't she? Given up everything for him and the children (ungrateful brats, she intimates). She speaks in the precise mid-Atlantic dialect that Hanrahan has come to associate with Canadian academic poseurs who've served their time in the UK. Once, describing a dead-end job she'd had, she uses the phrase "for my sins," but, Hanrahan thinks, quite clearly implies it was for someone else's sins, no doubt Bindle's. Perhaps she sees her entire life in such terms, he speculates.

The other women, by contrast, seem congenial, welcoming. Jane Grenberg is from South Dakota; the surname is Norwegian, not Jewish, in case Hanrahan was wondering. People up here often do. Jane's husband, Bill, is a grad student in Botany, working on a doctorate. They are married, though they have different last names, Bill's being so ridiculous—no kidding, it's "Victorious"— that she couldn't bring herself to change hers, unconventional as that seemed to her Dakota kin.

Hanrahan is charmed. He likes this refusal of victory, also the skepticism she expresses about the remedial program and Bindle. "He's always rushing off somewhere," she says. "Nobody would be surprised if he said, 'I must rush off and look at myself in the mirror for an hour.'" She does a fair imitation, given that she stands only about five-two, of Bindle's springing gesture, which seems to start at his toes and somehow propel him forward as well as upward, a specialized, unnatural sort of motion, as if he were competing in an obscure Olympic gymnastics event.

The other kindred spirit is Daphne Porter, early-to-mid-thirties, and "unattached," Jane confides. "Her boyfriend dumped her a couple of years ago, and she hasn't gotten over it." Her breath, Hanrahan will notice if he gets close enough, invariably smells of gin by mid-afternoon. "We don't know where she keeps it," Jane says. (Since the instructors share a large windowless room that serves as their office, there's no place to hide anything. Desk drawers would be risky: too many people coming and going.) "It's because of the boyfriend. What made it even worse was that he'd decided to become a monk. I mean, what a blow to your ego, right?"

None of this is discernible to Hanrahan in casual interaction with Daphne, but knowing these facts predisposes him to like her. And she, too, tends to roll her eyes at the mention of either of the Bindles. In Hanrahan's experience, shared irreverence is the fastest-acting bonding agent known to academe.

...

A week passes, the competency test is administered, the predictable fifty per cent failure rate is made public and deplored. Hanrahan and his fellow instructors spend two days interviewing their future students, going over their essays, explaining endlessly the nature of the comma splice, the sentence fragment, the dangling modifier, that *pons asinorum* of contemporary grammar. Most of the interviewees sit there mute and uncomprehending, politely tuning out Hanrahan's earnest, detailed justifications of their failure. (The students who passed were spared this ordeal.) Some express reactions ranging from outrage to amusement at the notion that grammatically correct sentences (a) exist and (b) are regarded as important by someone who can affect their lives. One young man actually whistles in surprise when Hanrahan explains the distinction between "lie" and "lay." "Never heard that one before," he says, almost reproachfully, as if Hanrahan (to whom credit for ingenuity had grudgingly to be given) had invented it to humiliate him.

This is the bottommost pit of hell, Hanrahan decides. Let's hope my Virgilian tour guide shows up soon.

Only one student manifests himself as an individual (as opposed to one of a crowd of interchangeable shades). Mr. Sweeney is angry. His essay has been failed, not because it is poorly written but because it is off-topic. How is this possible? The test required students to read a five-hundred-word passage of innocuous bumph about how wonderful universities are and then write their own "thoughts" (quotation marks Hanrahan's) about what "the university experience" might be like for them. Mr. Sweeney is probably the only person whose first language is English not to have attempted to do what was asked.

Mr. Sweeney's essay is about the inevitable global triumph of the communist revolution. The first paragraph features a rather florid evocation of the storming of the Winter Palace.

Hanrahan points out, as tactfully as he can, that there is no mention of what Mr. Sweeney hopes to accomplish at university.

Mr. Sweeney is a smallish young man with a crewcut and the sort of dark, baleful gaze that makes Hanrahan automatically think "sociopath."

"No one can accomplish anything worthwhile at a bourgeois institution such as this." Mr. Sweeney seems to be reading from an invisible teleprompter somewhere behind Hanrahan's left shoulder. "Except of course to contribute to its destruction."

"You must be the only Marxist in Alberta."

"I'm on the side of the evolution of humanity. That's all that matters."

Sweeney now glares directly at Hanrahan, as if expecting a physical attack by way of response.

"People like you would like to kill people like me." Sweeney says this dispassionately, a meteorologist reading the temperature.

"Mr. Sweeney, your existence is of no interest to me, one way or the other."

People like me, Hanrahan thinks. Authority figures. Capitalists. Agents of the degenerate status quo.

Sweeney hasn't responded. Clearly he was expecting an outburst of venom.

"This is hell, nor am I out of it," Hanrahan hears himself saying.

Sweeney blinks, plebeian Faustus, man of the people.

"Daddy owns an oil well, doesn't he?" says Hanrahan, going for the jugular.

But Sweeney recovers nicely. "My personal background is irrelevant."

A tense dialogue ensues, in which it develops that Sweeney has expected that his Marxist essay would be assigned to a devoutly Marxist faculty member, who would of course pass it. That is, he has heard, how things are done at universities.

All this is far in the past, and Hanrahan's life is much different now. Securely ensconced in the choir of the blessed, he can peer down through opera glasses into the inferno he once inhabited. He can watch his younger self stumble along what now seems a preordained route through the maze of exhibits in his personal museum of folly. It has its minor but real elements of fascination—like watching a miniseries about a war whose result is universally known but whose individual battles have long been forgotten.

Did Hanrahan actually say "This is hell, nor am I out of it" to Mr. Sweeney? Or is it merely important for him now to think that he did? If so, why? He's always suspicious of literary allusions and mythic references in the fiction he himself reads, imposing as they do a spurious tidiness on the incorrigible sprawl of experience.

• • •

Why does the person who lives across the hall from Hanrahan never appear in person? Why does he (or she: Hanrahan is quick to adapt to new verbal formulae, if not to the reality underlying them) constantly play music just loud enough to be discerned from the hallway, music that seems eerily out of date, top-forty hits from five years or so in the past: "Muskrat Love," for example, or "The Wreck of the Edmund Fitzgerald"? No doubt rational explanations are available. But what the hell would they be? And what about a good *irrational* explanation? Hanrahan allows the notion of time warp to flit through his mind (demented sparrow, fast-food banquet hall). In any case, the person in there, whether living or dead according to banal biological technicality, is in some sense stuck, transfixed, wriggling, pinned. As, from this multi-decades' long distance, Hanrahan himself may appear to be. But at the time he thinks how sad for someone to have condemned him/herself to hear the phrase "the big lake they call Gitche Gumee" over and over. At least, he remembers thinking back then, I'm not like that.

• • •

At least I'm not like that, Hanrahan thinks, not long after having been introduced to Bill Victorious. It's the Saturday evening after the encounter with Mr. Sweeney. Classes are to begin Monday. Jane has invited him for dinner; Daphne is there when he arrives.

Physically, Bill Victorious is unimpressive—Hanrahan's age, but he's balding, and his body seems wispy, barely present.

How his arms and legs are thin, Hanrahan thinks. But he's no Prufrock. He's got that American self-assurance radiating calmly from every pore. He speaks softly, with a self-effacing insistence in the tone. Every dialogue must lead to the conclusion that he is right about something; indeed (the tone says) it is in the natural order of things that he be right about *everything*. You have the right to disagree, but in so doing you will be making a fool of yourself. But don't worry; no one will laugh.

He has many anecdotes, all featuring himself. He refers to himself in the third person, sometimes as "Willy," then, much more annoyingly, as "Willy Lump-Lump"—a modest, simple sort of fellow who just happens to have the idea that solves the problem baffling his scientific colleagues. Often—within an hour Hanrahan feels that this adverb is justified—the anecdotes will begin with a general statement, such as "Roger is a pedant rather than a pedagogue." The generalization is explained on the basis of Roger's recent performance at a departmental colloquium. Since the subject of Roger's presentation seems to have been the chemistry of some aspect of a certain species of shrub, Hanrahan's attention wanders.

Why is Jane with this guy? he wonders. Jane is in fact gazing politely at her husband, unnaturally subdued. Daphne, though, is eager to make eye contact, taking mischievous pleasure in "Willy's" performance as she stares back at Hanrahan.

"So," Bill is saying, "the discussion was going nowhere fast, and then along comes Willy Lump-Lump asking 'Why don't you think of the problem *this* way?'" Hanrahan tunes out again. Is Daphne, just possibly...? He notes that Bill's voice is becoming somewhat excited, albeit in a controlled, laid-back sort of way. "And when he'd finished, there was a standing O for the Lumpster." Spoken as if marvelling at some long-ago feat of physical courage that he had once been privileged, by lucky accident, to witness. And also, as if half-expecting his three-person audience to follow suit.

Decades later, Daphne floats to the surface of Hanrahan's consciousness, round face and blue eyes, habitual ironic gleam laced with the absurd hope that alcohol has never quite defeated. "Why have you called me up? What do you want with me?"

I'm sorry, Hanrahan thinks. I have to make use of you. I'm trying to make sense of my life. That justifies pretty much anything these days. Are you alive or dead, by the way?

"Now or then?"

Hanrahan has no heart for this repartee. He has a nicely defined sense of what Daphne was all about. He doesn't need to think of what she may have become. Or have been.

He thinks about formulating a politician's statement concerning fondness or caring.

"Don't lie about me. Please. And don't pretend you've mis-remembered."

Gotta get out of this, Hanrahan thinks. This is starting to seem like Dido and Aeneas in the underworld.

"Aeneas? Give me a break. Gone off and founded a city, have you?"

Until this exchange, Hanrahan has forgotten the faintest trace of an English accent (from her parents; she's lived all her life in Calgary). He's forgotten that her father was a birdwatcher, and that Daphne and her brother once played a trick on him, attaching an elaborately detailed model of some seldom-seen species to a tree in their front yard, then drawing it to his attention. He'd watched it through his binoculars for half an hour before realizing that the bird was indeed absolutely motionless, and for good reason.

What is the purpose of Hanrahan's having retained this information?

"And don't forget," Daphne adds, "that when I was ridiculously too old for it, sixteen or seventeen, I'd go downtown and follow people selected at random, pretending I was a private detective. You found this fact to be characteristically depressing, like most information I gave you about myself, though pleased that I revealed it to you."

Hanrahan follows himself back several decades. Bill Victorious is discussing his research. He always hesitates slightly before pronouncing this word, as if to give it due reverence. His— research—involves the study of a certain plant, a fern that grows only in streams in the foothills of the Rockies. It has a double-barrelled Latin name, both words of which begin with "h." This plant has interesting, possibly unique properties. In winter, the h-h fern is, as it were, deader than dead, not merely your (pardon the pun, but do laugh in acknowledgement of Bill's wit) garden variety seasonal vegetal death, but real as-if-pulled-out-by-the-roots-and-microwaved-to-a-crisp death. Its comeback in the spring is thus a true resurrection. This word, too, is pronounced gingerly, as if Victorious were holding it at arm's length with a pair of tongs.

Don't worry, he's not going to bore his audience with a technical description—though for a moment he glances at Daphne, then at Hanrahan, as if to see whether they wouldn't, after all, demand to be bored—but it's starting to look as if ol' Willy Lump-Lump has stumbled on to what might fairly be called, in layman's terms, the secret of immortality.

This is what I'm supposed to become, Hanrahan is thinking. I'm supposed to have big, revolutionary ideas, convince myself that they're true, then convince the rest of the world that I'm right. "Wordsworth's Sonnets: The Key to Immortality." If I can't be Bill Victorious, I should do something else with my life. What, though?

It's later, and they've all had a fair bit to drink, except for the prissily abstemious Bill. The talk turns to the Bindles and the remedial writing program. Jane begins to come to life again, apparently with Bill's approval. (He can ease up, thinks Hanrahan, having, in his own mind, established dominance.) Hanrahan is initiated into many secrets involving his new colleagues. He himself tells the "boffo" story. All newcomers, he learns, are treated to some version of it.

"But the real story," Bill says, "is how or whether he boffos her."

Speculation about the Bindles' sex life is a conversational staple among remedial instructors. Their physical appearance cries out for mockery, both of them tall and thin, she with her expression of perpetual disgust, as if the entire world were composed of some form of unidentifiable animal excrement, and he with his complacent smile of foundationless self-regard. And they're such good targets for verbal caricature, their studied faux-Britishness making it all too easy to imagine Victorian dialogues: Rex protecting Amelia from exposure to spoken vulgarity ("Amelia, stop your ears!") only to be revealed, gradually, as sinister seducer, Amelia's maidenly reluctance gradually overcome by his foppish persuasion until, too late, the bestial nature of his desire is revealed ("No Rex, no, not the nether passage!").

Hanrahan feels somewhat uncomfortable at the enthusiasm with which both Jane and Daphne immerse themselves in this fantasy, also the way in which Bill encourages them to invent outrageous sexual detail. But how neatly the Bindles are paired, Hanrahan thinks, self-love and world-loathing, allegorical figures expressly designed to illuminate something, damned if he can get a handle on what.

This is the sort of perception that Hanrahan associates with excessive consumption of alcohol. He decides that he has licence to take one potentially shit-disturbing shot, since the evening will soon be drawing to a close.

"What always puzzles me," he ventures, "is how egomaniacs like Bindle always manage to find intelligent—if in this case flawed in other respects—women like Amelia to play second fiddle to them." Of course Hanrahan is also speaking of Bill and Jane, a fact that he knows, somehow, Daphne will pick up on.

Hanrahan has in fact wondered about this one since he was fifteen. His initial hypothesis—that egomaniacs have huge dicks—was dispelled by empirical locker room investigation. But he hasn't since found a convincing replacement.

Jane is eager to tell him. "Women," she begins, effortlessly presenting herself a spokesperson for her entire gender (in Hanrahan's experience, a common rhetorical move among drunken females), "women would like nothing better than to cavort, cavort, cavort." Hanrahan has already heard her use this apparently idiosyncratic euphemism (or is it commonplace in the Dakotas?). "But," she says, and pauses to stare at him. "You, babycakes, have all the power."

Hanrahan isn't sure which has surprised him most: the word "babycakes," the word "power," or the bold, inviting nature of her stare.

• • •

Half a lifetime later, Hanrahan remembers Daphne saying to him, that evening or some other, "All men are weak." Hanrahan, as it happened, was the case in point. The tone has stayed with him as much as the content—nothing of anger, reproach, regret, disappointment, simply an acknowledgement of a fact of nature: water flows downhill; the sun rises in the east; all men are weak. Thank you, Daphne. I've kept that bit of wisdom in my hip pocket all this time. It's worth having around.

• • •

The night unfolds with inexorable logic. It has been established that Daphne's apartment is not that far from Hanrahan's and that it will therefore be convenient for them to share a cab (the Grenberg-Victorious ménage is off in some other part of town, geographically unidentifiable to Hanrahan at this point). The cab will go by Daphne's place first. She will invite him in for a nightcap, as if either of them needs it. One thing will lead to another.

But what about Sharon? Some of you are asking. (Nearly all of you are women.) Has Hanrahan forgotten about her? (No.) Has he then made a calculated decision to attempt to be unfaithful to her? (Not exactly.) What, then? Well, this is a separate reality. In this parallel universe, Sharon exists only as an abstraction, a Platonic Ideal, let's say. She's real in one sense, but she's not, well, *there*. No point in bruising the body to pleasure soul is how Hanrahan looks at it. "...*that was in another country / and* besides, *the wench is dead.*" And so forth.

In the cab, Hanrahan tells Daphne about his encounter with Mr. Sweeney.

"Sweeney Agonistes," Daphne says.

"Annoying as he was, there was something engaging about him. He was so sure that he was right."

"You're making him sound like Bill Victorious."

"Did he really say at one point, 'Plants can't move, but they have rich and complex lives nonetheless'?"

"I'm afraid he did. She'll leave him. She's not ready yet. She doesn't even know it yet. But it's just a matter of time."

Daphne does invite Hanrahan in for a nightcap. They estimate it will take him no more than fifteen minutes to walk home afterward.

They're in the apartment, drinks in hand. What are those drinks, anyway? She on the sofa, he in an armchair. Skirt sliding up, inadvertent, but no corrective action taken. Good sign. Hanrahan has rarely seen a female thigh he couldn't stare at for hours.

Somehow the existence of Sharon makes its way into the conversation.

"Ah, the Intended," Daphne says. "I knew there would be one. There always is."

"The what?"

"Intended. As in *Heart of Darkness*, Kurtz and that crowd."

"I thought you said 'the Offended.'"

"That, too, perhaps."

"I like the image of me as Kurtz, though. Professor Kurtz-Hanrahan, hunched over a stack of essays, muttering 'The horror! The horror!'"

"Don't bother telling me about her. They all sound more or less the same."

The drink and the talk seem to collaborate in binding them together, sweet illusion of intimacy or maybe the real thing, who's to say, certainly not Hanrahan.

What he does become sure of, soon enough, is that Daphne is the loneliest person he's ever met. She's had no relationships since being dumped, at least none that last longer than a night. She doesn't seem to have friends anymore, either. She's not sure what happened. People move away or they get married or they have all-consuming careers. Some of the people at work are nice, but not her type. Jane, for example, is good-hearted but naive and bland. So there are weekends when Daphne doesn't leave her apartment. Most days the only phone call she gets is from her mother, precisely at six p.m., to make sure that she's still alive. The only mail she gets is bills; once she sent an envelope to herself so that she could simulate the experience of getting a personal letter. She drinks more than she should, as Jane has doubtless told him. A single man who lives in the apartment across the hall is constantly propositioning her, but he's an illiterate lout. She has a collection of pornography, but she won't insult Hanrahan by showing it to him—"pictures of people in crotchless underwear doing silly things to each other."

At a certain point Daphne is doing something at the sink. Rinsing? Mixing? Hanrahan comes over to her. It seems natural to stand there, as if to be ready to offer assistance, and then, gently, he hopes, to take her breasts in his hands, thumbs brushing nipples through the fabric of her blouse. Unsurprised, she continues to rinse (or mix).

"You can stay," she says.

In the distant future, Hanrahan contemplates what happens then, though he is now bereft of the shield of alcohol that protects him from any immediate sense that he is betraying both Sharon and Daphne. Though Daphne would deny it, would claim total responsibility for her own actions, and though no Marlow will travel to Vancouver to tell Sharon that Hanrahan has become Kurtz.

Nevertheless, Hanrahan wonders, is this the first (though not last) instance of unfaithfulness that is the seed that will burst into perverse bloom more than a decade later when his and Sharon's marriage will teeter on the brink of failure? Who knows what occult concatenation of cause and effect comes into play in such situations? Perhaps this was it, the chomping of the apple as the cock crows thrice and the thirty pieces of silver jingle in his pocket. Hanrahan is still enough of a Catholic to entertain such thoughts.

• • •

Like Tiresias who has foresuffered all, Hanrahan returns to the scene of the misdemeanour.

To Daphne's breasts, firm and high, revealed and proffered without fanfare or coyness.

To Daphne's bed, where, yes, there is mention of Rex and Amelia Bindle, a jokily necessary distancing ritual.

Yes, there is more sadness as Daphne reveals that she has never come with a man inside her, that heroic efforts by Hanrahan are unnecessary, that this feels good and that doesn't, but the end as it were will not be achieved by any means, no not orally either, thanks. Which is not to say that there is no pleasure or passion on her part, let her demonstrate, let talking cease except for necessary operational instructions and requests. And yes, there is, anomalously, passion, Hanrahan amazed by her wriggling energy and then his own, mercifully swallowed by the epiphany of flesh, he to be praised later (as if by a spectator sport's old pro colour commentator) and the Intended (not wistfully but matter-of-factly) declared a lucky woman.

"Boffo," Daphne says when Hanrahan comes.

Squinting back and down across the years through his expensive opera glasses (he's paid plenty), Hanrahan concludes smugly that he behaved as he did because that is what people do when they are in hell.

HANRAHAN
SAVED

t's the end of the seventies, and Hanrahan is trying to teach himself how to teach. He's in Vancouver, a grad student in English, and this is his summer job—a community college, but not a regular course, not even a regular division of the college, but something called Special Programs. It's not at the standard community college level—it's for students who don't "fit into" the public high school system and want to get the equivalent of Grade Twelve, an equivalent that will be recognized by someone, somewhere. Special Programs isn't sure that this will be true of the course Hanrahan is teaching.

Hanrahan doesn't care. He likes teaching, likes these students better than the first-year university crowd he's familiar with, thirty bland-blank faces knowing damn well all they need do is sit there and make sure their assignments are handed in to get their obligatory first-year credit.

The Special Programs bunch is different. They don't all work hard, but they want their money's worth, they'll tell you what they like and don't like, they have opinions (however ill-founded): they're alive.

There are about fifteen of them. Hanrahan sees them for four hours a day, in a windowless room somewhere in the bowels of the Special Programs building: too much time together, so Hanrahan runs as loose a ship as possible, which is what he'd be inclined to do anyway. If your assignment is late, well, these things happen. If you haven't done the required reading, go over in the corner and do it now, while the rest of us carry on. Interrupting Hanrahan is encouraged. Generous chunks of class time are used for doing homework. Hanrahan likes to congratulate himself on his liberalism in these matters.

He isn't quite sure what he's supposed to be teaching, but he doesn't care. The course is called Canadian Viewpoints, which label covers a mélange of literature, history, sociology, political science, you name it (as long as it's Canadian). There's no official curriculum, no standard course outline, no prescribed texts. The last person to have taught the course has disappeared from Special Programs without a trace. Hanrahan is on his own.

He makes do, he survives, he enjoys it. "You can't spend that much time with a group of people and not like them," Hanrahan tells himself and others. He has no idea whether the class is learning anything, but he certainly is. What he's learning about, mostly, is them.

On the first day, it's the ones who are most obviously different who catch his attention: Elmer, who's legally blind; Annie, the dark girl whose top is so skimpy it borders on indecency; Brad, the loud one who seems to have a chip on his shoulder, and whom Hanrahan is sure he has seen selling dope at a Doobie Brothers concert; Jason, with his crew cut, jacket and tie; and Kimberly, a self-possessed young woman who approaches Hanrahan at the end of the class to tell him that she is a born-again Christian and that this fact will probably manifest itself in everything she writes for the course.

That, too, is fine with Hanrahan. Whatever turns you on. As long as it's related to the course, a concept that expands a little each day. Before long, he knows most of the others too. They hang around after class. They call him at home. They go for coffee with him. They confide in him. Peter, who's thirty, won't be in on Tuesday because he's trying to get custody of his son and has to attend a hearing. Sylvia is having trouble with her boss at the fast-food restaurant—he keeps trying to grab her in a back room, and she needs the job. What does Hanrahan suggest? Malcolm is convinced that he's being followed through the streets by a Chinese man who's waiting for the opportunity to proposition him or (on some days) to attack him physically in unspecified but heinous ways.

"How big is he?"

"About five-two, sir. Weighs about one-twenty. Short hair. Standard facial features. No visible scars or other identifying marks."

Malcolm's ambition is to join the police force. His own stats, Hanrahan guesses, would be about six-two, one-eighty.

"Don't you think you'd be big enough to defend yourself if he did attack?"

"He almost certainly has martial arts expertise, sir."

Hanrahan wouldn't trade this sort of thing for the world. He has several conversations with Malcolm, who, he guesses, simply wants someone to listen to him. After a time, the mysterious Chinese man seems to disappear from Malcolm's life. I must be doing okay, Hanrahan tells himself.

As he does when he notices that Brad has stopped trying to be disruptive, as he does when Sheila tells him she's decided to ditch the boyfriend who's responsible for her chipped tooth. "Our talk about that helped a lot," she says. Hanrahan feels a warm glow radiating from somewhere in his gut, wallows in the recognition that he's participating in a satisfying cliché.

Not that he neglects academics, not at all. Within a few days he recognizes that these students, by and large, don't read very well, aren't used to concentrating. So he has them read things aloud, paragraph by paragraph, essays and short stories from the texts he's ordered, more or less at random, before the course started. It helps. They stop to discuss things, in detail. The ones who are self-conscious about reading aloud are encouraged by the others.

Hanrahan thinks he can identify the moment at which the class comes together, becomes a team. They're reading a story. At a certain point it dawns on Hanrahan that, four paragraphs ahead, one character will call another a "son of a bitch" several times, and that the person due to read it is Kimberly, the born-again Christian, who has in a low-key but gently firm way already made known her views on such topics as abortion, pornography, drug use, premarital sex—and foul language. One paragraph ahead, some of the other students notice it, too. Nudges, fingers pointing, brief whispers. Too late to intervene. Today Kimberly is wearing a sweatshirt that says "Open Bible Institute" on it. And then she is saying, miraculously, with soft conviction: "Son of a bitch… son of a bitch."

An important symbolic gesture, Hanrahan would try to explain to those of his friends who would listen. She was declaring herself to be in some way *a member of the class*, willing to subordinate her own preferences to the needs of the group. And the others sensed this, subliminally, maybe, and perhaps for the first time realized that the class *was* a community you could belong to. Hanrahan believes that they all feel that way—all except Estelle.

Estelle is different, different in a way that the other different ones are not. Estelle Shapiro, the only Jewish student in the class. An attractive young woman, but there's something strange about her. Not that she's a "problem" in any conventional sense. She's bright, does her work, gets good grades. Never volunteers an answer, speaks only when required to read aloud, never speaks, as far as Hanrahan can gather, to her classmates. The only one who has refused to acknowledge any sense of community.

She does nothing overt to draw attention to herself, Hanrahan thinks, but you notice her just the same. She dresses differently from the other girls, for example. It's a hot summer, and most days everyone wears as little as possible. None of the other girls, with the exception of Kimberly, can be counted on to wear a bra on any given day. They favour tank tops, tee shirts, short shorts, cut-off jeans, light summer dresses. A casual glance around the room will usually register Estelle as an island of darkness in a maelstrom of bright colours. (The other exception is Jason, whose jacket has disappeared, though his white shirt and tie have remained—he wants to be a stockbroker, he's told Hanrahan, a profession that requires a certain formality of attire, he believes.) In any case, black is Estelle's favourite colour. She tends to wear long, flowing dresses with high necklines, the proper attire for a solemn, dignified hippie, Hanrahan thinks—a hippie under-taker, perhaps. She wears bright red lipstick, most days. Entering or leaving class, she moves slowly but purposefully, a clipper ship gliding toward some exotic port, oblivious to the chatter around her.

Once, toward the end of the third week—the course is to run for six—Hanrahan tries to make contact, asking her to stay for a moment after class. He compliments her on a paper she's written, an analysis of a poem, which includes a particularly impressive interpretation of a difficult, convoluted metaphor.

"How did you come up with that?" (Hanrahan couldn't have thought of it himself.)

She looks at him for a few seconds, doubtfully, as if trying to decide whether the cards should be laid on the table. Hanrahan thinks that she may be about to confess to plagiarism.

"I don't know," she says. "I was in a trance when I wrote this paper."

This line delivered with a total absence of insolence, no hint of mockery.

"A trance," Hanrahan repeats, knowing as he does it that he probably sounds like a zombie himself.

"That's not unusual for me, Mr. Hanrahan. May I go now?" Hanrahan nods, convinced that she's telling the truth. He thinks for a moment of calling her back, but decides against it.

But Estelle comes back to him, the next week, of her own accord. Hanrahan is a bit ashamed of how it happens, a bonus for a gesture of simple decency on his part.

It's a hot afternoon, as usual. Hanrahan has taken the class outside, onto the front lawn of the Special Programs building. This procedure is frowned upon by Ms. Genevieve Butterfield, director of instruction, but not actually forbidden. In Hanrahan's opinion, Ms. Butterfield is somewhat wacko anyway. She has a tendency to end their brief, one-way conversations by saying, "It's a dirty game we're playing here at Special Programs. A dirty game and a nasty game. And it's going to get dirtier and nastier." She says this with considerable relish. Hanrahan has no idea what she means and thinks it better not to ask.

In any case: a hot afternoon, the class sprawled in a semicircle on the lawn, half of them daydreaming no doubt, but what the hell, Hanrahan thinks, they might as well be doing it outside as in. And at least half of them seem interested in the discussion, which has moved of its own accord from Canada's participation in World War II to a general consideration of the Holocaust. Kimberly is making the point that many Christians were murdered by the Nazis, not only Jews, even though the Jews seem to get all the attention in the history books. They showed a movie at her church only last week in which—

And at this point Brad intervenes, Brad who is showing signs of reverting to his first-week rebelliousness, apparently having realized that Hanrahan will eventually require him to produce a token amount of work if he's going to pass this course, and that he, Brad, is just not up to it, not this summer. But he needs to stay in the course to keep on the good side of his probation officer, who checks with Ms. Butterfield, who checks each week with Hanrahan. So Brad has to sit there in class, aware that his dream of one day doing Phys Ed at UBC is receding farther and farther into the realm of the highly improbable. Brad, in other words, is pissed off, and decides to take it out on Hanrahan by saying:

"I figure those six million Jews that got fried must've deserved it, don't you?" And he glares at Hanrahan, his blue eyes stereotypically Aryan, Hanrahan realizes; he even has blond hair.

Hanrahan waits for a moment. Everyone is paying full attention now. And Hanrahan is in his glory. He could hug Brad for giving him this opportunity. There are many things that someone like Hanrahan can say in response to a remark like Brad's, and Hanrahan finds himself saying some of them with considerable eloquence and force, if he does say so himself.

When he's finished, God knows how long later, he asks if there are any questions. Silence. Brad is staring at the ground, pulling up little tufts of grass. Some of the others are staring at Brad. Most are staring at Hanrahan, who announces that class is dismissed for the day, twenty minutes early. And to hell with Ms. Butterfield, who even now is poking her long nose out her office window, like a nocturnal rodent whose den has been rocked by a mid-afternoon tremor.

Next day, at the end of class, Estelle waits patiently for Hanrahan to deal with two other students so that she can tell him how much she appreciated what he said yesterday, how the things he'd said were exactly what she'd wanted said under those circumstances. And then she apologizes for being so curt and cryptic the other day—it's just that it happens to be the truth, this business about writing essays in a trance state, but no one ever believes her. But she thinks the only way to deal with people is to be as honest as possible, that's her policy, and if they can't handle it, that's their problem. But now she realizes that Hanrahan is a decent person, she shouldn't have been so quick to assume otherwise. If he's interested, she can tell him more, a lot more.

"Let's go for coffee," Hanrahan says.

Estelle is from the east, from Ontario, like Hanrahan himself. Her parents are divorced. She's living with an aunt in Vancouver, but she's going back to Ontario at the end of the summer. From the time she was a small child, she's been aware that she's different from other people. It's not just the thing about the trances. She's into astral projection, for example. For her, it's as normal as taking a Number Ten bus along Granville to get downtown. And she meets spirits in this realm of soul travel—the spirit of her dead grandfather, for one. And she knows a thing or two about the forces of darkness and the forces of light.

Hanrahan has never met anyone like Estelle. She seems sane. The experiences that she describes are clearly real—for her. She's bright, she seems to be in touch with the everyday reality inhabited by the likes of Hanrahan, she has a sense of humour, seems not to be paranoid or megalomaniac, seems in fact to be as sane and balanced a person as Hanrahan knows, despite the weird things she tells him.

What is Hanrahan to make of this? His view of the world can easily accommodate Kimberly and Brad, whose deviations from his vague, genial notion of normalcy are predictable, safe. But here is a sane young woman who lives in a world of complete otherness. How does one respond?

"Tell me about this astral projection. What's it like?" And she does tell him, prefacing everything by saying that any description will be misleading, because we're dealing with a metaphysical region in which words are unnecessary, superfluous, a place where reality is intrinsically paradoxical, if that makes sense. (It doesn't, but Hanrahan nods.) A place where there is light, but a dark light. A place that is without dimension. A place that is inside you as much as outside you, a place where you're a participant in everything, not an observer of everything outside the self. A place where the concept of time is irrelevant. And so on.

Hanrahan is fascinated, not so much by the details—which are, in the end, incomprehensible to him—but by the sense of conviction that comes across from Estelle. She's really been there, wherever "there" is.

Judge not, Hanrahan. Different strokes. And yet a part of him regrets that Estelle's life has been like this. And what part of you is that, Hanrahan? The part of you that would deny freedom to others, the part of you that wants to be dictator of the universe?

Estelle in fact seems perfectly happy to be what she says she is. (But then why the dark clothing? And why the eagerness to talk to Hanrahan now?) And it's a good thing she's not asking for help, isn't it? What would you recommend, Hanrahan? Cold showers? Exorcism? This is a long way from Sheila and her boyfriend, from Malcolm and his non-existent Chinese predator.

Speaking of Sheila, here she is, sitting beside Hanrahan on the bus on their way home. This happens two or three times a week, and Hanrahan welcomes it. Sandra and Estelle are brighter, but Sheila is his favourite. She was a street kid, a runaway, for a couple of years in early adolescence (a time she doesn't like to talk much about), but somehow she's managed to come through it. At seventeen, she's got energy, ambition, a good sense of herself. Hanrahan admires the hell out of her and wonders how he would have done himself in parallel circumstances. And besides, her hair is the exact auburn shade of Hanrahan's own. They could be brother and sister.

So Hanrahan is mildly alarmed when Sheila says, "Some of us are getting a bit worried about you."

"Why?"

"Well, we've noticed that Estelle seems to be hanging around you a lot lately, going for coffee and such. I know that's your business"—here she makes a gesture to prevent Hanrahan from interrupting—"but, you know, there's something weird about her, maybe even something"—here she hesitates, searching for the right word—"evil."

"Give me a break."

"No, listen. I'll tell you something that happened the first week, when most of us didn't know each other at all. One day before class Brad was bugging Estelle, asking her out and stuff, kidding around the way guys do. And then he said something that must have pissed her off, and she just stared at him for a few seconds and Brad sort of crumpled, I mean fell down on his ass really hard. And Estelle just turned and sort of floated away, you know the way she does." (An edge of irony here, Hanrahan notes. Is Sheila jealous?)

"So what," he says. "That was Brad being a clown. Nothing new about that."

"No. That's what we thought, at first. But then Brad said that when Estelle stared at him, he just felt all the strength going out of his body? Like he couldn't even put his hands out to break his fall? I've never seen Brad that serious."

"So what do you think?"

"I think she's got some kind of evil power. I think maybe she's like a vampire or something."

"I'll watch out for her fangs."

"It's not a joke."

"I'll be careful," says Hanrahan, patting her shoulder in what he hopes is an avuncular manner.

But try as he might, Hanrahan can discern no trace of evil in Estelle. Then, in the last week of the course, she intimates that she has something more to tell him, something of a different order entirely.

"Do you believe in UFOs?" she asks him.

"I've never seen one myself," says Hanrahan, "but I'm certainly open to the idea that they exist." Is he? Of course he is. Hanrahan is open to everything, on principle, he believes.

"Well," Estelle goes on, "I don't think they're from outer space or anything. I think they're from some kind of parallel universe. Not really aliens. I just think of them as the Others, with a capital 'O.' I think they want to help us, to bring peace to our world."

"The... Others?"

Estelle and Hanrahan are walking along Kitsilano Beach at sunset. She has suggested the time and place—it's somewhere, she's said, where they can keep moving and so can't possibly be interrupted. He likes sunsets, especially dramatic ones like these, the sun plunging recklessly behind Hollyburn, leaving a delicate, idiosyncratic spectrum of colours behind it. Just now there's a strip of fast-fading orange-juicy light along the top of the ridge. The sea is dead calm.

"Yes. The Others," Estelle says. "They've—been in touch with me." And she turns to look Hanrahan in the eye. She's really lovely, Hanrahan thinks. In the Jewish American Princess tradition, top of the line. Why does she seem not to have a boyfriend? And why has he not asked himself that before? Pay attention, Hanrahan. What she's saying is important to her.

And she tells what Hanrahan will come to recognize, as he educates himself in this subject over the next decade or so, as the standard contactee story. This first incident, she says, occurred several years ago. She was by herself at the family cottage in Ontario. Her parents had gone to a party on the other side of the lake. She went for a walk along the shore. Then: a strange aircraft overhead, a landing in a field a hundred yards from where she was walking, a blinding flash of light, paralysis, telepathic communication with a group of four-foot-high creatures in silver jumpsuits, bald humanoids with enormous dark hypnotic eyes, thin noses, a slit for a mouth, no discernible ears. They took Estelle on board their craft, did some kind of testing with scientific or medical instruments, took a blood sample, Hanrahan can see the scar on the back of her left calf (here she raises the hem of her dress, and there it is, a long faint red mark that could, Hanrahan thinks, have been caused by anything).

Anyway, when they'd finished with their tests, they told Estelle (still telepathically) that the people of her world were in danger of destroying themselves and that she, Estelle, had been chosen to play a major role in helping to avert catastrophe. She would be given more information about this as time went on. All she needed to know for the moment was that all human religions were wrong about almost everything, except for Buddhism, which had a higher batting average than most, and that reincarnation was a fact, so she should not fear death. (Wait a minute, Hanrahan thought, we're in danger of destroying ourselves but we're all going to be reincarnated anyway, so we can't really destroy… Shut up, Hanrahan, she's on a roll.)

And, true to their word, they *had* contacted her several times since, on each occasion telling her more about their plans for her in the struggle for world peace.

"They've told me," she says, her own dark hypnotic eyes riveted on Hanrahan, who has to glance away after a moment, "they've told me that I will do more than any other human being to help save the world."

The last of the orange light leaks away from the ridge of Hollyburn. Hanrahan turns back to Estelle. He thinks, I am peering into the perfectly composed face of a beautiful young woman who happens to be mad. This is what madness is, Hanrahan. Note it well.

It wears the mask of sanity, but do not be deceived. She lives on the other side of the line over which you must not cross.

And Hanrahan smiles and says something encouraging, sympathetic, the way he always does.

Soon the course is over. The final exam is worth only ten per cent, so there's no pressure there. Brad slinks out early, less than a page written in his booklet. As they leave the room, most of the students make a point of saying goodbye to Hanrahan. Elmer confides that *Never Cry Wolf* is the first book he's ever actually read, cover to cover. Peter has failed to get custody of his son, but he's going to keep trying. Annie will be taking courses at Special Programs in the fall—is there any chance that Hanrahan will be teaching there again? (No.) Jason, tie loosened for the occasion, says that Hanrahan wasn't bad at all as an instructor, he's had lots worse. (Thanks, Jason.) Sheila, Kimberly, and Estelle all promise to keep in touch.

Estelle's goodbye is quick. She and Hanrahan haven't spoken privately since their walk along the beach. She'll be moving back east sooner than she'd thought, probably within a week, so they won't have time to talk again. But she'll write.

And so Hanrahan goes back to the rest of his life. There's his dissertation, of course, which he hasn't had time to work on during the last six weeks. And there's Sharon, his live-in girl-friend, who, Hanrahan suspects, is about to become increasingly important. Sharon is a grad student, too, further advanced than Hanrahan, smarter, more highly motivated. The size of her fellowship makes it unnecessary for her to take a job during the summer. She'll have her dissertation completed and examined by this time next year.

What does she see in Hanrahan? He hasn't a clue, but he's happy that she's around. In a year or so he'll be proposing marriage like it's no big deal. And she'll say Yes, with some enthusiasm. He just knows it.

Weeks pass, months. Sheila does keep in touch. She becomes a full-time babysitter with a family near the main campus of the college (Special Programs rapidly fading in her rear-view mirror), takes night courses, finds a new boyfriend, gains self-confidence. She and Hanrahan meet for coffee every few weeks. He always comes away feeling good about her, himself, the system (whatever that means), the universe. Score one for our side, he thinks.

Kimberly is a different story. In the fall she gets married suddenly and moves to Cranbrook. She writes two letters to Hanrahan. In the second, she says that this will have to be the end of their correspondence, because her husband thinks it inappropriate for her to be writing to another man. Fred is a good husband, she says, a god-fearing born-again Christian like herself, but he doesn't understand why she likes to spend so much time reading books other than the Bible, so she supposes she'll have to cut back on that. If you ever want to learn about self-sacrifice, she adds, try getting married. God bless you, Hanrahan—who thinks, Oh well, you can't win 'em all.

Meanwhile, he and Sharon are getting along just fine. After a time, he notices certain ominous phrases creeping into her conversation—phrases like "getting settled" and "biological clock." They're both "well past" twenty-five, she'll point out at frequent intervals; thirty will be upon them before they know it. No problem, thinks Hanrahan to himself; it's not like we'll wake up tomorrow and suddenly be thirty, is it? This is good stuff. I'll go along with this. More time passes.

And from Estelle Shapiro he hears not one word.

•••

It's somewhat more than ten years later. The Hanrahan who once taught at Special Programs has long since passed on and been replaced by a new-model Hanrahan, one who has, reptile-like, shed the energy and idealism he once wore like a skin. He's not sure what has replaced them. What has happened to

Hanrahan? There are many answers to this question. The fourth decade of his life has happened to him. The eighties have happened to him.

Specifics, please. Well, Hanrahan and Sharon are married. They have an eight-year-old daughter, Mary Catherine. The name was Hanrahan's idea. In a time when so much about one's identity is "problematic," he argued, making sure that Sharon could hear the scare quotes, it's best to give her something to hang onto: Mary Catherine Hanrahan—no doubt as to what kind of person *she* is. "But Hanrahan," Sharon objected at the time, "you're only one-quarter Irish and I'm not Irish at all." But Hanrahan stood firm on this one, and in the end he prevailed.

In any case. The Hanrahan family has moved to Ottawa, his hometown. Both adults have deserted academe (or it, them). Sharon is on the brink of the civil service equivalent of stardom. She's well up in the SX bracket, though Hanrahan couldn't tell you what her job title is, or even which government department she's in (the names keep changing, and she keeps moving). She works in one of the gleaming new government buildings downtown; he knows that. Every now and then she explains, again, what it is that she actually does—but he forgets almost immediately. What he doesn't forget is that she keeps moving up, though he's not sure what's at the top.

And Hanrahan? He works, too, but his office is at home. He writes. He writes reports of various kinds for government departments and agencies. He's a hired gun. Sometimes he's in complete control of a project from formulating the concept to

the finished product. Sometimes it's simply a matter of turning some bureaucrat's barbarism into clear English. Sometimes
it's something in between. Hanrahan is good at this work, and
makes more than decent money at it, but he knows it's not what
he was born to do. And what *were* you born to do, Hanrahan?
Well, he's not sure what, exactly.

But this isn't it. On his bad days, occasionally he'll sit at his
computer and let his fingers magically cause the sentence "You
are a whore" to appear on the screen. This is the truth, Hanrahan
will tell himself. An honest whore, one who gives good value
for the money, one who even, from time to time, enjoys certain
aspects of the work—but a whore nonetheless. Let's not kid
ourselves.

Is Hanrahan desperately unhappy, then? No, that's not true.
His marriage, for example, is in pretty good shape, considering.
Sharon is the only completely honest adult he's ever known, and
as he gets older, he's more and more impressed by this. And
whatever it is that brought them together in the first place is
still there in some form, mutated perhaps, or simply muted—
but surfacing now and then in a certain kind of eye contact,
arm-squeeze, shared joke at the world's expense, unexpected
half-hour that approximates passion. They're still together.
Hanrahan's not complaining, no sir.

And then there's Mary Catherine, the real centre of his life
now, he sometimes thinks. Once, out drinking with the two high
school buddies with whom he keeps in touch, he heard himself
saying, incredibly, "If it weren't for Mary Catherine, I don't think

196 · LARRY MATHEWS

there'd be any point to my life at all. I don't think I'd even want to go on with it." He was horrified to think that he could say this. Could it be true? Probably not. No, certainly not. It was the beer talking, not Hanrahan. And in any case, wasn't it just a negative way of putting something that might better be phrased in terms of his deep, powerful love for his daughter?

His only daughter, only child. The one major political issue dividing him and Sharon these days. He wants another one. Now he's the one who talks about the biological clock. And she says that she agrees in principle, but these days many women are having babies well into their forties—give her another year or two, one more rung up the ladder, and then she'll give the idea every consideration.

But still. On balance, in the main, is this not something one could call a reasonably happy life? As defined, that is, by the norms appropriate to Hanrahan's age, class, economic bracket? This is a fallen world, Hanrahan. Remember what the nuns taught you in grade school—not in the same building, but in a reasonable facsimile of the one to which you've insisted on sending Mary Catherine. Hanrahan can never get the name straight. He thinks it might be Immaculata, or something like that. He's made this decision, he tells himself, on the grounds that when the time comes, at least she'll have something tangible to rebel against; no argument from Sharon. Anyway, they knew something, those nuns, about how rotten the world is, and how we're all implicated in its rottenness, original sin and so forth. Be content, Hanrahan, with whatever happiness you can find in this vale of tears. You're in better shape than most, console yourself with that. And stop whining.

Very occasionally, Hanrahan will think of Estelle Shapiro. He has of course given up hope of ever hearing from her. But he still thinks that he may one day hear *of* her, a thirty-second clip on *The National* about the leader of a tiny UFO cult declaring the advent of the millennium, Estelle smiling discreetly in the background perhaps, too independent-minded, Hanrahan would fantasize, to herself aspire to leadership with its messy organizational issues. She'd be a hanger-on, sure, but ready to bolt if the mood struck her. Hanrahan has no idea why he has made this story up, what bizarre need it must satisfy.

So yes, Hanrahan has not entirely forgotten Estelle. In fact he has, over time, made a modest attempt to educate himself in the disreputable field of UFOlogy. He knows, now, for example, that there is a significant correlation between psychic ability of the sort apparently possessed by Estelle, and the likelihood of alleged contact with aliens. (Hanrahan himself doesn't have a psychic bone in his body, a fact for which he's more and more grateful, the more he thinks about it.) He knows, too, that Estelle's description of her initial encounter was classical, almost suspiciously so—but that there is a tendency for contactees to forget or repress parts of their experience, or to alter details. He knows that the notion of aliens as bringers-of-world-peace, using chosen humans as their prophets and PR people, is pretty commonplace too, as these things go. One common denominator: the "aliens" (if that's what they are; Hanrahan remembers

Estelle saying she believed they were from a parallel interdimensional world, not outer space) *never tell the truth*. The "prophecies" never come true. The goal of the Others, as Estelle called them, is to confuse and mislead rather than to enlighten and help. Hanrahan doesn't know what to make of the whole phenomenon but tries, as usual, to keep an open mind.

The Hanrahans live in the Glebe, in a three-storey house on a quiet street not far from the Canal—another sign that they're doing okay, better than okay, financially. Maybe next year they'll have a deck added at the back. Hanrahan's workplace is a third-storey bedroom facing the street. He can beaver away at his computer and, for diversion, keep tabs on the action in the neighbourhood. Sometimes he's inexplicably happy when he's alone in the house like this, Sharon off in her office tower, Mary Catherine at school, Hanrahan in a world of his own.

One warm morning in late May, Hanrahan is working at his latest assignment. This is not one of the more interesting ones. His task is to put into coherent English a brief on the plastics industry, the first draft of which was written by a bureaucrat named René Paquette, who indicated cheerfully over the phone that, although he himself is in fact perfectly bilingual, his boss has strongly suggested that Hanrahan should have a look at what he's written before it goes to the minister's office. Hanrahan is in the process of giving it a preliminary once-over. For ten minutes now, he's been reading this sentence: "There is a feeling that this highly diversified industry has led to the uneasy identification of the lowest common denominator among this heterogeneous set, which does not provide a good canvas upon which could be embroidered a net scene with the right perspective for all the elements and a dominant tone, suggestive of the bottom line on competitiveness."

No wonder the country is so fucked up, Hanrahan thinks. On the other hand, it might be worse if we did understand each other. The document, he knows, is intended to provide advice to the minister about how to make public statements on the plastics industry. And Hanrahan just might bet that René Paquette knows exactly what he's doing. Listen to sentences like that, and you can find in them whatever you like. If the minister says something that he thinks is in accordance with René's advice and it backfires, René can always claim that his prose has been misinterpreted. Perhaps Hanrahan's wisest course of action here is to let well enough alone—skim the document, bill René's boss for the time it would have taken to read it thoroughly, and recommend that the report be forwarded as written. (And isn't that a better way to earn one's living than by making a fool of oneself in front of a roomful of bored nineteen-year-olds? You've chosen well, Hanrahan.) On the other hand something in him wants to twist the sentence into meaningfulness, longs for clarity, for—if this doesn't sound too pompous—truth.

It's a good morning for staring out the window. There's greenness everywhere along Hanrahan's street—lawns, shrubs, hedges, trees. It's the time of year when women are wearing noticeably less than they did two or three weeks ago, and Hanrahan rejoices in this fact when he gets the chance. Birds sing. The sun shines. Hanrahan is in his simulacrum of heaven, gazing down at the world.

And then a woman leaves the house directly opposite Hanrahan's, a woman he has seen before but never really noticed until now. This woman is, Hanrahan thinks, what Sharon might call "striking" or possibly "stunning." What that means for Hanrahan is that her appearance inspires aesthetic appreciation rather than lust. This woman is graceful, verging on willowy, wearing the sort of dress that Sharon might wear to work—except it's black. She could be about thirty. Her facial expression, insofar as Hanrahan can interpret it, is businesslike.

And he has, of course, a sense that he has seen her before, long before she moved in across the street, whenever that was— probably the first of the month. When was it, the previous time? And before long he has made the connection that you, reader, have no doubt already made. He believes that his new neighbour bears a strong resemblance to Estelle Shapiro—or at least, Estelle Shapiro as she might have evolved over the past decade and a half or so. (It can't be almost two decades, can it?)

Hanrahan keeps his eyes peeled for the rest of the morning, and all afternoon, but he doesn't think she came back. Next morning, though, he has his binoculars ready, and sure enough, at exactly the same time, she emerges. She stops for a moment and looks around, as if expecting someone to pick her up. Hanrahan gets a good look at her. It's Estelle, all right, or her twin sister. Close up, her face seems more sad than businesslike today, something about the set of the mouth, something about the eyes.

Then she's on the sidewalk moving toward the nearest bus stop, with the same stately gliding motion that Hanrahan remembers from Special Programs, though now it suits her better, seems more natural. As she disappears around a corner, Hanrahan notes that a black van with illegible lettering on its side moves off in the same direction.

Estelle Shapiro. A certain kind of reader will draw back here, will withhold something, will complain to the management about "contrivance" or "unconvincing use of coincidence." Such readers, I would suggest, have not been paying attention to their own experience. Have there not been times, reader, possibly more times than you'd care to admit to yourself, when the uncanny has managed to get its foot inside *your* front door, its larger-than-life foot inside its big weatherbeaten workboot?

Of course it has not yet been proved that the woman in question *is* Estelle Shapiro. Hanrahan is sure of it, but what if she denies it? (Why would she, Hanrahan wonders, and why am I even thinking that?) She's obviously rented the house across the street. The Petersons' house. Bert Peterson works for some agency, CIDA perhaps, though he's not sure, that has posted him somewhere in Africa for a year. So that's why the house was on the rental market, but what is Estelle *doing* here? How can you save the world if you live in Ottawa? Shouldn't the aliens (excuse him, the "Others") have commanded her to go public by now? Or—and this idea fills Hanrahan with disappointment the moment he conceives it—what if she's aborted the mission? What if she's become *one of us*? She leaves the house in the late mornings because she has a flex-time job designing computer programs for the Defence Department, or crunching numbers at

StatsCan, or inventing new ways to deprive people of EI, or any of a thousand similar fates Hanrahan wouldn't wish on anyone. Welcome to Ottawa yuppiedom, Estelle. Where's your Volvo? We go to a Club Med in the Caribbean for a week in February. We have cottages in the Gatineau or up the Valley somewhere. You'll like it here. Everyone on our street eats well. Many of us have shrinks. We've all got American Express. Forget those silly old "Others" and dig in.

On the third morning, Hanrahan is ready. He peeks out the front door. If you open yours, Estelle, I'll open mine. She does. He does. Like figures on a cuckoo clock, they pop out onto their respective front steps. But today something different happens. Estelle makes a dash for the curb, jumps into a black Buick Skylark Hanrahan has never seen before and screeches off, burning rubber. Followed immediately by the same black van Hanrahan has noted before, a black van with glass you can't see through. And lettering Hanrahan still can't quite make out as it speeds past, defying the laws of the physics of van acceleration. Or so it seems to him.

Hanrahan, you will have noticed, does not observe Estelle when she returns from wherever she goes. Oh, he glances out the front window in the evenings more than he usually does, but he's made no systematic attempt at surveillance. The reason, of course, is Sharon. There's no way that Hanrahan can explain to her the depth and intensity of his interest in their new neighbour. It's easy enough for her to become suspicious of *any* woman who passes briefly through the margins of Hanrahan's life. No point in drawing her attention to this one. Still, on this third night (or night of the third day?), he wills himself to stay awake after Sharon has drifted off. At two a.m., he's looking out the window. No lights at Estelle's, but the now familiar black van is in its usual place, present and accounted for.

"Hanrahan, what are you doing at the window? It's the middle of the night."

"Nothing, babe," Hanrahan thinks of replying. "I was just checking to see if any UFOs have landed on Estelle's lawn, you know Estelle, she's my former student from way back when, in Vancouver, who's mysteriously moved in across the street, and she's being watched by somebody in a van who may be from CSIS, or possibly the CIA, or they may just possibly be from another dimension, a parallel universe. In which case they're not really 'aliens,' though that's what most people would call them." No, Hanrahan thinks, better not try. "I thought I heard something out there," he does say.

Morning number four. The appointed hour comes and Estelle does not appear. The van is still there. Hanrahan waits five minutes, ten. Why not take the initiative. He's out the door and across the street before he lets himself think of good reasons not to. Rings her bell. "Hi, my name is Hanrahan? From across the street? You know, you remind me a lot of a young woman I taught in a class in Vancouver? About maybe fifteen years ago?" What could be more innocent. But there's no answer.

Okay, next check out the van. For one thing, he can now read the lettering on the side. Macdonald and Cartier. Exterminators. No address. No phone number. Yeah, sure, exterminators.

Hanrahan has sometimes watched *Miami Vice*. Mary Catherine is a fan. He recalls that Don Johnson's underlings do their surveillance work using this cover; though, being flamboyant Americans, they have a huge replica of an insect on the roof of their van. And note the names here—some oversight committee with a mandate to enforce biculturalism must have devised it. So at least they're *ours*. Unless of course…

The glass of the windshield and door windows reflect Hanrahan's image back at him. He taps gently on a window. No response. He walks around to the other side. Here the lettering reads: Cartier et Macdonald. Exterminateurs.

Hanrahan goes back inside. Half an hour later, a black Skylark appears at the curb in front of *chez* Hanrahan. A man wearing a military uniform is getting out and walking toward the front door. Ringing the bell. Be ready.

The military man turns out to be pasty-faced, bland-featured. Later Hanrahan won't be able to remember what he looked like at all.

But there's something strange about the uniform.

"Mr. Houlihan?"

"Hanrahan," says Hanrahan.

"Hanrahan, right, yes, of course, excuse me. May I come in for a moment? It's… government business."

Hanrahan hesitates. Yes, let him come in, get him talking, no telling what he might spill. He doesn't look too bright. He doesn't know that Hanrahan knows… Wait a minute, Hanrahan, what *do* you know?

The military guy says his name is Colonel somebody but doesn't say the surname clearly enough for it to register as an actual name. No doubt a deliberate strategy, Hanrahan concludes, when he thinks about it later.

"Mr. Hanrahan, we've noticed you... taking an interest... in the van down the street."

The uniform, Hanrahan realizes. He hasn't seen one like it since the armed forces were unified, years ago. Is it the old army uniform? (Hanrahan wouldn't have a clue.) It looks brand new—one of the weird, apparently pointless anachronisms associated with many accounts of encounters with "the Others." And is that what this is? Really?

"...young woman who lives across from you." The visitor is continuing, "matter of national security... asking for your co-operation... rely on the loyalty of patriotic citizens." He delivers this speech in a bored, sing-song voice. He's looking somewhere above and behind Hanrahan. He gives the impression of having done this many times before.

This may be my only chance, Hanrahan thinks. Better go for it. He breaks rudely into the Colonel's spiel. "Where are you from?" he says loudly. "I mean, is it like another dimension? A parallel universe? Or what?"

The Colonel looks confused for a moment, then chuckles. Maybe he's human after all, Hanrahan thinks. Surely only humans would chuckle? Ignoring the interruption, the Colonel continues, in a more conventionally conversational tone. "I know, Mr. Hanrahan. To ordinary citizens it must seem as if we're from another planet. But we have a serious job to do, let me assure you. And we need all the help we can get from civilians such as yourself. Please don't try to get involved in this, sir. Believe me, it's better not to know."

He turns and lumbers out the door, stopping briefly to thank Hanrahan for having heard him out. It's a good act, Hanrahan thinks. Unless of course he really is someone from our version of the secret police after all. Maybe he's not one of the Others. Maybe Hanrahan should take everything he's said at face value. Maybe...

Another hour or so passes without incident, Hanrahan glued to the window. Then Estelle emerges, begins walking down the street, away from the van, whose engine, predictably enough, bursts into life.

Hanrahan waits until she's almost at the corner, then he's out the door and after her. He stays about half a block behind. Meanwhile the van is crawling along about two car lengths behind *him*. Estelle is heading for Bank Street, not looking back. Hanrahan picks up the pace. So does the van.

At Bank Street, she's into a supermarket, Hanrahan moving faster behind her. He thinks back to Special Programs, to Sheila's warning.

Watch out, Hanrahan. We think she may be evil. No, little sister of the streets, Hanrahan can deal with this, whatever it is.

Inside, Hanrahan trots up and down the aisles, cartless, jostling shoppers, some of whom look at him, puzzled, placid as cattle grazing in the shade. There she is, over by the meat.

There's the Colonel, down the way, fondling sausages, glancing over anxiously at Estelle every two seconds.

The voice of Malcolm in Hanrahan's head: he almost certainly has martial arts expertise, sir.

Courage, Hanrahan. "Estelle? Estelle Shapiro? Remember a long time ago in Vancouver, on Kits Beach at sunset you told me that the Others said you were going to help save the world? It's me, Hanrahan, your teacher... your friend."

Estelle has been looking down, looking away (at what? What is she actually doing?). But now she faces Hanrahan. The same eyes he remembers, but changed. Eyes that speak of suffering, eyes that, Hanrahan thinks he discerns, have confronted evil and not been overcome by it. Eyes lit not by madness but by something benign. From somewhere in his scholarly past, the phrase "benignant light" comes to mind, some Romantic poem read only by Hanrahan and the half-dozen other students in that grad seminar, a poem in which someone's eyes prevent someone from fleeing because of their benignant light. At the same time something makes Hanrahan aware of his own conclusion about the Others: *They never tell the truth. They always lie and mislead. Always.*

But Estelle is surely not in league with them. Look at the eyes, Hanrahan.

Finally Estelle is speaking. "Mr. Hanrahan," she's saying. "I've seen you with your wife, your daughter. You have a good life. Be content with the good things in it." But Hanrahan already knows that this is good advice. He doesn't need Estelle to tell him that.

208 • LARRY MATHEWS

"Never mind," he says. "*What are you up to?* I mean, are you supposed to be saving the world or what?"

"Mr. Hanrahan, I have seen things, I have known things there is no need for you to see or to know. Things impossible to describe. Enjoy the world as you understand it."

Think fast, Hanrahan. "One thing I have to know. Please. You're not with them, are you? I mean on the side of the Others? Remember you said they'd chosen you? Is that still true, I mean do you still believe that?"

"Mr. Hanrahan, this conversation must end. Please leave the store." A command, not a request. A sphinx-like smile, if there is such a thing.

The store fluorescent lights, all of them, flicker off and then on again—even brighter than before? And Hanrahan remembers the story about Brad keeling over when Estelle looked at him the wrong way.

"Go in peace, Mr. Hanrahan."

Hanrahan knows that he will never see her again, knows that she will never again return to the house across the street, that Sharon will not remember her at all, that the attempts that he will surely make to track her down will hit dead ends. But none of this matters, as Hanrahan walks, projecting some semblance of dignity, he hopes, out into the glorious sunshine. He believes. Hanrahan believes!

As for exactly what he believes, please don't ask him just yet. He's not entirely sure himself. Of course it has something to do with Estelle. But not Estelle as Our Lady of the UFOs. No, that path would lead nowhere. It's more the sense that the world is other than what Hanrahan had assumed it was, a bigger, brighter, richer and more mysterious place. A place where Hanrahan can perhaps, one day, discover what he *was* really born for. He has no idea how to do that, but he's going to devote his life to finding out. From now on, he promises himself. Because, he's now certain, he was definitely born for something.

ACKNOWLEDGEMENTS

Thanks to everyone at Breakwater for making this book happen. And especially, thanks to my life's partner, Claire Wilkshire, for her unfailing patience, kindness, and love.

Editor—Shelley Egan
Copy editor—Claire Wilkshire
Cover design—Rhonda Molloy
Proofreader—Geoff Pevlin